The Cloven Viscount

BOOKS BY ITALO CALVINO

The Baron in the Trees

The Castle of Crossed Destinies

The Cloven Viscount

Collection of Sand

The Complete Cosmicomics

Difficult Loves

Fantastic Tales

Hermit in Paris

If on a winter's night a traveler

Into the War

Invisible Cities

Italian Folktales

Marcovaldo

Mr. Palomar

The Nonexistent Knight

Numbers in the Dark

The Road to San Giovanni

Six Memos for the Next Millennium

Under the Jaguar Sun

The Uses of Literature

The Watcher and Other Stories

Why Read the Classics?

ITALO CALVINO

The Cloven Viscount

Translated from the Italian by

ARCHIBALD COLQUHOUN

marinerbooks.com

First published in Italy as *Il visconte dimezzato* by Einaudi, Turin, 1951.

Library of Congress Cataloging-in-Publication Data is available.
ISBN 978-0-544-96006-0

Printed in the United States of America
23 24 25 26 27 LBC 9 8 7 6 5

The Cloven Viscount

I

There was a war on against the Turks. My uncle, the Viscount Medardo of Terralba, was riding towards the Christian camp across the plain of Bohemia, followed by a squire called Kurt. Storks were flying low, in white flocks, through the thick, still air.

"Why all the storks?" Medardo asked Kurt. "Where are they flying?"

My uncle was a new arrival, just enrolled to please ducal neighbors involved in that war. After fitting himself out with a horse and squire at the last castle in Christian hands, he was now on his way to report at Imperial headquarters.

"They're flying to the battlefields," said the squire glumly. "They'll be with us all the way."

The Viscount Medardo had heard that in those parts a flight of storks was thought a good omen, and he wanted to seem pleased at the sight. But in spite of himself he felt worried.

"What can draw such birds to a battlefield, Kurt?" he asked.

"They eat human flesh too, nowadays," replied the squire, "since the fields have been stripped by famine and the rivers dried by drought. Vultures and crows have now given way to storks and flamingos and cranes."

My uncle was then in his first youth, the age in which confused feelings, not yet sifted, all rush into good and bad, the age in which every new experience, even macabre and inhuman, is palpitating and warm with love of life.

"What about the crows then? And the vultures?" he said. "And the other birds of prey? Where have they gone?" He was pale, but his eyes glittered.

The squire, a dark-skinned soldier with a heavy moustache, never raised his eyes. "They ate so many plague-ridden bodies, the plague got 'em too," and he pointed his lance at some black bushes, which a closer look revealed were not made of branches, but of feathers and dried claws from birds of prey.

"One can't tell which died first, bird or man, or who tore the other to bits," said Kurt.

To escape the plague exterminating the population, entire families had taken to the open country, where death caught them. Over the bare plain were scattered tangled heaps of men's and women's corpses, naked, covered with plague boils, and, inexplicably at first, with feathers, as if those skinny legs and ribs had grown black feathers and wings. These were carcasses of vultures mingled with human remains.

The ground was now scattered with signs of past battles. Their progress slowed, for the two horses kept jibbing and rearing.

"What's the matter with our horses?" Medardo asked the squire.

"Signore," he replied, "horses hate nothing more than the stink of their own guts."

The patch of plain they were crossing was covered with horses' carcasses, some supine with hooves to the sky, others prone with muzzles dug into the earth.

"Why all these fallen horses round here, Kurt?" asked Medardo.

"When a horse feels its belly ripped open," explained the squire, "it tries to keep its guts in. Some put bellies on the ground, others turn on their backs to prevent them from dangling. But death soon gets 'em all the same."

"So mostly horses die in this war?"

"Turkish scimitars seem made to cleave their bellies at a stroke. Further on we'll see men's bodies. First it's horses, then riders. But there's the camp."

On the edge of the horizon rose the pinnacles of the highest tents, and the standards of the Imperial army, and smoke.

As they galloped on, they saw that those fallen in the last battle had nearly all been taken away and buried. There were just a few limbs, fingers in particular, scattered over the stubble.

"Every now and again I see a finger pointing our way," said my uncle Medardo. "What does that mean?"

"May God forgive them, but the living chop off the fingers of the dead to get at their rings."

"Who goes there?" said a sentinel in a cloak covered with mold and moss, like a tree bark exposed to the north wind.

"Hurrah for the Holy Imperial crown!" cried Kurt.

"And down with the Sultan!" replied the sentinel. "Please, though, when you get to headquarters, do ask 'em to send along my relief, because I'm starting to grow roots!"

The horses were now at a gallop to escape the clouds of flies surrounding the camp and buzzing over heaps of excrement.

"Many's the brave man," observed Kurt, "whose dung is still on the ground when he's already in heaven," and he crossed himself.

At the entrance they rode past a series of canopies, beneath which thick-set women with long brocade gowns and bare breasts greeted them with yells and coarse laughter.

"The pavilions of the courtesans," said Kurt. "No other army has such fine women."

My uncle was riding with his head turned back to look at them.

"Careful, Signore," added the squire, "they're so foul and pox-ridden even the Turks wouldn't want them as booty. They're not only covered with lice, bugs and ticks, but even scorpions and lizards make their nests on them now."

They passed by the field batteries. At night the artillerymen cooked their ration of turnips and water on the bronze parts of swivel guns and cannons, burning hot from the day's firing.

Carts were arriving, full of earth, which the artillerymen were passing through sieves.

"Gunpowder is scarce now," explained Kurt, "but the soil of the battlefields is so saturated with it that a few charges can be retrieved there."

Next came the cavalry stables where, amid flies, the veterinarians were at work patching up hides with stitches, belts and plasters of boiling tar, while horses and doctors neighed and stamped.

The long stretches of infantry encampments followed. It was dusk, and in front of every tent soldiers were sitting with bare feet in tubs of warm water. As they were used to sudden alarms night and day, they kept helmet on head and pike tight in fist even at foot-bath time. Inside taller tents draped like kiosks, officers could be seen powdering armpits and waving lace fans.

"That's not from effeminacy," said Kurt, "just the opposite. They want to show how they're at ease in the rigors of military life."

The Viscount of Terralba was immediately introduced into the presence of the Emperor. In his pavilion, amid tapestries and trophies, the sovereign was studying future battle plans. Tables were covered with unrolled maps and the Emperor was busy sticking pins in them, taking these from a small pincushion proffered by one of the marshals. By then the maps were so covered with pins that it was impossible to understand a thing, and to read them, pins had to be taken out and then put back. With all this pinning and unpinning, the Emperor and his marshals, to keep their hands free, all had pins between their lips and could only talk in grunts.

At the sight of the youth bowing before him, the sovereign let out a questioning grunt and then took the pins out of his mouth.

"A knight just arrived from Italy, Your Majesty," they introduced him. "The Viscount of Terralba, from one of the noblest families of Genoa."

"Let him be made lieutenant at once."

My uncle clicked spurs to attention, while the Emperor gave a regal sweep of the arm and all the maps folded in on themselves and rolled away.

Though tired, Medardo went to sleep late that night. He walked up and down near his tent and heard calls of sentries, neighs of horses and broken speech from soldiers in sleep. He gazed up at the stars of Bohemia, thought of his new rank, of the battle next day, of his distant home and of the rustling reeds in its brooks. He felt no nostalgia or doubt, or apprehension. Things were still indisputably whole as he was himself. Could he have foreseen the dreadful fate awaiting him, he might have even found it quite natural, with all its pain. His eyes kept straying towards the edge of the dark horizon where he knew the enemy camp lay, and he hugged himself with crossed arms, content to be certain both of the distant and differing reality, and of his own presence amidst it. He sensed the bloodshed in that cruel war, poured over the earth in innumerable streams, reaching even him, and he let it lap over him without feeling outrage or pity.

2

Battle began punctually at ten in the morning. From high on his saddle Lieutenant Medardo gazed over the broad array of Christians ready for attack, and raised his face to the wind of Bohemia, swirling with chaff like some dusty barn!

"No, don't turn round, Signore," exclaimed Kurt, now a sergeant, beside him. And to justify the peremptory phrase he murmured, "It's said to bring bad luck before battle."

In reality he did not want the Viscount to feel discouraged, for he knew that the Christian army consisted almost entirely of the line drawn up there, and that the only reinforcements were a few platoons of rickety infantry.

But my uncle was looking into the distance, at an approaching cloud on the horizon, and was thinking: "There, that cloud contains the Turks, the real Turks, and these men next to me, spitting tobacco, are veterans of Christendom, and this bugle now sounding is the attack, the first attack in my life, and this roaring and shaking, this shooting star plunging to earth and treated with languid irritation by veterans and horses is a cannon ball, the first enemy cannon ball I've ever seen. May it not be the day when I'll say—'And it's my last.'"

Then, with bared sword, he was galloping over the plain, his eyes on the Imperial standard vanishing and reappearing amid the smoke, while friendly cannon balls rotated in the sky above his head, and enemy ones opened gaps in the Christian ranks and created umbrellas of earth. "I'll see the Turks! I'll see the Turks!" he was thinking. There's no greater fun than having enemies and then finding out if they are like one thought.

Now he saw them, saw the Turks. Two came right up, on mantled horses. They had round little leather shields, black and saffron striped robes, turbans, ocher-colored faces and moustaches, like someone at Terralba called "Micky the Turk." One of the two was killed and the other killed someone else. But now numbers of them were arriving and the hand-to-hand fighting began. To see two Turks was to see the lot. They were soldiers, too, all in their own army equipment. Their faces were tanned and tough, like peasants'. Medardo had seen as much as he wanted to of them. He felt he might as well get back to Terralba in time for the quail season. But he had signed on for the whole war. So on he rushed, avoiding scimitar thrusts, until he found a short Turk, on foot, and killed him. Now that he had got the hang of it he looked round for a tall one on horseback. That was a mistake, for small ones were the most dangerous. They got right under horses with those scimitars and hamstrung them.

Medardo's horse stopped short with legs splayed. "What's up?" said the Viscount. Kurt came up and pointed downwards. "Look there." All its guts were hanging to the ground. The poor beast looked up at its master, then lowered its head as if to browse on its intestines, but that was only a last show of heroism; it fainted, then died. Medardo of Terralba was on foot.

"Take my horse, Lieutenant," said Kurt, but did not manage to halt it, as he fell from the saddle, wounded by a Turkish arrow, and the horse ran away.

"Kurt!" cried the Viscount, and went to his squire, who was groaning on the ground.

"Don't think of me, sir," said the squire. "Let's hope there will be some schnapps in the hospital. A can is due to every wounded man."

My uncle Medardo flung himself into the melee. The fate of battle was uncertain. In the confusion it seemed the Christians were winning. They had certainly broken the Turkish lines and turned some of their positions. My uncle with other bold spirits even got close up to the enemy guns as the Turks moved them to keep the Christians under fire. Two of the Turkish artillerymen were pivoting a cannon. With their slow movements, beards, and long robes, they looked like a pair of astronomers. My uncle said, "I'll see to them." In his enthusiasm and inexperience he did not know that cannons are to be approached only by the side or the breech. He leapt in front of the muzzle, with sword bared, thinking he would frighten the two astronomers. Instead of which they fired a cannonade right in his chest. Medardo of Terralba jumped into the air.

After dusk, when a truce came, two carts went gathering Christian bodies on the battlefield. One was for the wounded and the other for the dead. A first choice was made on the spot. "I'll take this one, you take that." When it looked as if something was salvageable, they put the man on the wounded cart; where there was nothing but bits and pieces they went on the cart of the dead, for decent burial. Those who hadn't even a body were left for the storks. In the last few days, as losses were growing, orders had been given to be liberal about wounded. So Medardo's remains were considered those of a wounded man and put on that cart.

The second choice was made in the hospital. After battles the field hospital was an even ghastlier sight than the battle itself. On the ground were long rows of stretchers with poor wretches in them, and all around swarmed doctors, clutching forceps, saws, needles, amputated joints and balls of string. From body to body they went, doing their very best to bring every one back to life. A saw here, a stitch there, leaks plugged, veins turned inside out like gloves and put back with more string than blood inside, but patched up and shut. When a patient died whatever good bits he still had in him went to patching up another, and so on. What caused most confusion were intestines; once unrolled they just couldn't be put back.

When the sheet was pulled away, there lay the Viscount's body, horribly mutilated. It not only lacked an arm and leg, but the whole thorax and abdomen between that arm and leg had been swept away by the direct hit. All that remained of the head was one eye, one ear, one cheek, half a nose, half a mouth, half a chin and half a forehead; the other half of the head was just not there. The long and short of it was that just half of him had been saved, the right part, which was perfectly preserved, without a scratch on it, except for that huge slash separating it from the left-hand part blown away.

How pleased the doctors were! "A fine case!" If he didn't die in the meantime they might even try to save him. And they gathered round while poor soldiers with an arrow in the arm died of blood poisoning. They sewed, kneaded, stuck; who knows what they were up to. The fact is that next day my uncle opened his only eye, his half mouth, dilated his single nostril and breathed. The strong Terralba constitution had pulled him through. Now he was alive and half a man.

3

When my uncle made his return to Terralba I was seven or eight years old. It was late, after dusk, in October. The sky was cloudy. During the day we had been working on the vintage, and over the vine rows we saw approaching, on the gray sea, the sails of a ship flying the Imperial flag. At every ship we saw then we used to say, "There's Master Medardo back," not because we were impatient for his return, but in order to have something to wait for. This time we guessed right; and that evening we were sure, when a youth called Fiorfiero, who was pounding at the grapes on top of the vat, cried, "Ah, look down there!" It was almost dark and down in the valley we saw a row of torches being lit on the mule path. Then when the procession passed the bridge we made out a litter borne by hand. There was no doubt; it was the Viscount returning from the wars.

The news spread through the valley. People gathered in the castle courtyard: retainers, domestics, vintagers, shepherds, men at arms. The one person missing was Medardo's father, old Viscount Aiolfo, my grandfather, who had not been down to the courtyard for ages. Weary of worldly cares, he had renounced the privileges of his title in favor of his only son before the latter left for the wars. Now his passion for birds, which he raised in a huge aviary within the castle, was beginning to exclude all else. The old man had recently had his bed taken into the aviary too, and in there he shut himself, and didn't leave it night or day. His meals were handed through the grill of the cage together with the bird seed, which Aiolfo shared. And he spent his hours stroking pheasants and turtle doves, as he awaited his son's return.

Never had I seen so many people in the courtyard of our castle; gone were the days, which I'd only heard about, of feasts and neighbors' feuds. For the first time I realized how ravaged were the walls and towers, and how muddy the yard where we now foddered goats and filled troughs for pigs. As they waited, all were discussing in what state the Viscount Medardo would return. Rumors had reached us some time before of grave wounds inflicted by the Turks, but no one quite knew yet if he was mutilated or sick or only scored by scars. At the sight of the litter we prepared for the worst.

Now the litter was set on the ground, and from the blackness within came the glitter of a pupil. Sebastiana, his old nurse, made a move towards it, but from the dark came a raised hand with a sharp gesture of refusal. Then the body in the litter was seen to give angular and convulsive movements, and before our eyes Medardo of Terralba jumped to the ground, leaning on a crutch. A black cloak and hood covered him from head to foot; the right-hand part was thrown back, showing half his face and body close against the crutch, while on the left everything seemed hidden and wrapped in edges and folds of that ample drapery.

He stood looking at us, at the silent circle surrounding him, but maybe he was not looking at us out of that fixed eye at all, perhaps he just was lost in his own thoughts. A gust of wind blew from the sea and a broken branch on top of a fig tree groaned. My uncle's cloak waved, and the wind bellowed it out, stretched it taut like a sail. It almost seemed to be passing through the body as if that body was not there at all, and the cloak empty, like a ghost's. Then on looking closer we saw that it was clinging to him like a standard to its pole, and this pole was a shoulder, an arm, a side, a leg, all leaning on the crutch. The rest was not there at all.

Goats looked at the Viscount with fixed inexpressive stares, each from a different direction, but all tight against each other, their backs arranged in an odd pattern of right angles. Pigs, more sensitive and quick-witted, screamed and fled, bumping their flanks against each other. Even we could not hide our terror; "Oh my boy," cried old Sebastiana and raised her arms. "You poor little thing!"

My uncle, annoyed at making such an impression, advanced the point of his crutch on the ground and with a hop began pushing himself towards the castle entrance. But sitting cross-legged on the steps of the great gate were the litter bearers, half-naked men with gold earrings and crests and tufts of hair on shaven heads. They straightened up and one man with plaits who seemed their leader said, "We're waiting for our pay."

"How much?" asked Medardo, almost laughing.

The man with the plaits said, "You know the tariff for carrying a man in a litter . . ."

My uncle pulled a purse from his belt and threw it, tinkling, at the bearer's feet. The man quickly weighed it in a hand, and exclaimed, "But that's much less than we'd agreed on, Signore."

Medardo, as the wind raised the edges of his cloak, said, "Half."

He brushed past the litter bearer with little jumps on his single foot and went up the stairs, through the great open gate giving on to the interior of the castle, pushed his crutch at both the heavy doors which shut with a clang, and then as the wicket gate remained open banged that too and so vanished from our eyes. We continued to hear the alternating tap of foot and crutch from inside, moving down passages towards the wing of the castle where his private apartments lay, and also the banging and bolting of doors.

His father stood waiting behind the grill of the bird cage. Medardo had not even paused to greet him. He shut himself into his rooms alone, and refused to show himself or reply even to Sebastiana who knocked and sympathized for a long time.

Old Sebastiana was a big woman dressed in black and veils, her red face without a wrinkle except for one almost hiding her eyes. She had given milk to all the males of the Terralba family, gone to bed with all the older ones, and closed the eyes of all the dead ones. Now she went to and fro between the apartments of the two self-imposed prisoners, not knowing what to do to help them.

Next day, as Medardo gave no more sign of life, we went back to our vintaging, but there was no gaiety, and among the vines we talked of nothing but his fate, not because we were so fond of him but because the subject was fascinating and strange. Only Sebastiana stayed in the castle, listening attentively to every sound.

But old Aiolfo, as if foreseeing that his son would return so glum and fierce, had already trained one of his dearest birds, a shrike, to fly up to the castle wing in which were Medardo's apartments, then empty, and enter through the little window of his rooms. That morning the old man opened the bird-cage door to the shrike, followed its flight to his son's window, then went back to scattering bird seed to magpies and tits, and imitating their chirps.

A little later he heard the thud of something flung against the windows. He leant out; there on the pediment was the shrike, dead. The old man took it up in the palms of his hands and saw that a wing was broken off as if someone had tried to tear it, a claw wrenched off as if by two fingers, and an eye gouged out. The old man held the shrike tight to his breast and began to sob.

That same day he took to his bed, and attendants on the other side of the cage saw that he was very ill. But no one could go and take care of him, as he had locked himself inside and hidden the keys. Birds flew around his bed. Since he had taken to it they had all refused to settle or stop fluttering their wings.

Next morning, when the nurse put her head into the bird cage, she realized that the Viscount Aiolfo was dead. The birds had all perched on his bed, as if it were a floating tree trunk in the midst of sea.

4

After his father's death Medardo began leaving the castle. Sebastiana was the first to notice when one morning she found his doors flung open and his rooms deserted. A group of servants was sent out through the countryside to follow the Viscount's path. The servants, hastening along, passed under a pear tree which they had seen the evening before loaded with tardy, still unripe, fruit. "Look up there," said one of the men; they stared at pears hanging against a whitish sky, and the sight filled them with terror. For the pears were not whole, but were cut in half, down the middle, and were still hanging on their own stalks. All there was of every pear was the right side (or left, according to which way one looked, but they were all on the same side) and the other half had vanished, cut or maybe eaten.

"The Viscount has passed by here!" said the servants.

Obviously, after being shut up without food for so long, he had felt hungry that night and climbed up the first tree he saw to eat pears.

As they went the servants met half a frog on a rock, still

alive and jumping with the vitality of frogs. "We're on the right track!" and on they went. But they soon lost it, for they missed half a melon among the leaves, and had to turn back until they found it.

So they passed from fields to woods and saw a mushroom cut in half, an edible one, then another, a poisonous red *boletus,* and as they went deeper into the wood kept finding every now and again mushrooms sprouting from the ground on half a leg and with only half an umbrella. These seemed divided by a neat cut, and of the other half not even a spore was to be seen. They were fungi of all kinds, puff balls, ovules and toadstools—and as many were poisonous as eatable.

Following this scattered trail, the servants came to an open space called "The Nun's Field," with a pool in the middle of the grass. It was dawn and on the edge of the pool stood Medardo wrapped in his black cloak looking at his reflection in the water, on which floated white, yellow and dun-colored mushrooms. They were the halves of the mushrooms he had carried off, scattered now on that transparent surface. On the water the mushrooms looked whole, and the Viscount was gazing at them. The servants hid on the other side of the pool and did not dare say a thing, but just stared at the floating mushrooms, until suddenly they realized that those were the edible ones. Where were the poisonous ones? If he had not flung them into the pool, what could he have done with them? Back the servants set off through the woods at a run. They did not have to go far because on the path they met a child carrying a basket, and inside it were all the poisonous halves.

The child was myself. That night I had been playing alone around the Nun's Field giving myself frights by bursting out of trees, when I met my uncle hopping along by moonlight over the field on his one leg, with a basket on his arm.

"Hullo, Uncle!" I shouted. It was the first time I was able to call him that.

He seemed vexed at the sight of me. "I'm out for mushrooms," he explained.

"And have you got any?"

"Look," said my uncle and we sat down on the edge of the pool. He began choosing among the mushrooms, flinging some in the water, and dropping others in the basket.

"There you are," said he, giving me the basket with the ones he had chosen. "Have them fried."

I wanted to ask him why the basket only contained halves of mushrooms, but I realized that the question would have been disrespectful and ran off, after thanking him warmly. I was just going to fry them for myself when I met the group of servants, and heard that all my halves were poisonous.

Sebastiana the nurse, when I told her the story, said, "The bad half of Medardo has returned. Now I wonder about this trial today."

That day there was to be a trial of a band of brigands arrested the day before by the castle constabulary. The brigands were from our estates and so it was for the Viscount to judge them. The trial was held and Medardo sat sideways on his chair chewing a fingernail. The brigands appeared in chains. The head of the band was the youth called Fiorfiero who had been the first to notice the Viscount's litter while pounding grapes. The injured parties appeared: they were a group of Tuscan knights who were passing through our woods on their way to Provence when they had been attacked and robbed by Fiorfiero and his band. Fiorfiero defended himself saying that those knights had come poaching on our land and he had stopped and disarmed them as poachers, since the constabulary had done nothing about them. It should be said that at the time assaults by brigands were very common, and laws were clement. Also, our parts were particularly suitable for brigandage, so that even some members of our family, especially in these turbulent times, would join brigand bands. As for smuggling, it was about the lightest crime imaginable.

But Sebastiana's apprehensions were well founded. Medardo condemned Fiorfiero and his whole band to die by hanging, as criminals guilty of armed rapine. But since those robbed were guilty of poaching he condemned them to die on the gibbet too. And to punish the constables who had appeared too late and not prevented either brigands or poachers from misbehaving, he decreed death by hanging for them too. There were about twenty altogether. This cruel sentence produced consternation in us all, not so much for the Tuscan gentry whom no one had seen until then, as for the brigands and constables who were generally well liked. Master Pietrochiodo, packsaddle-maker and carpenter, was given the job of making the gibbet. He was a most conscientious worker who took great pains in all he did. With great sorrow, for two of the condemned were his relations, he built a gibbet ramificating like a tree, whose nooses all rose together, and were maneuvered by a single winch. It was such a big and ingenious machine that it could have hanged simultaneously even more people than those now condemned. The Viscount took advantage of this to hang ten cats alternating with every two criminals. The rigid corpses and cats' carcasses hung there for three days, and at first no one had the heart to look at them. But soon people noticed what a really imposing sight they were, and our own judgments and opinions began to vary, so that we were even sorry when it was decided to take them down and dismantle the big machine.

5

For me those were happy times, wandering through woods with Dr. Trelawney in search of fossil traces. Dr. Trelawney was English; he had reached our coasts after a shipwreck, astride a ship's barrel. All his life he had been a ship's doctor and made long and perilous journeys, some of them with the famous Captain Cook, though he had seen nothing of the world since he was always under hatches playing cards. On being shipwrecked among us he soon acquired a taste for a wine called *cancarone,* the harshest and heaviest in our parts, and now could not do without it, so that he always had a full water flask of it slung over his shoulder. He had stayed on at Terralba and become our doctor; but he bothered little about the sick, only about his scientific researches, which kept him on the go—and me with him—through fields and woods by day and night. First came a crickets' disease caught by one cricket in a thousand and doing no particular harm. Dr. Trelawney wanted to examine them all and find the right cure. Next it was specimens of the time when our lands were covered by sea, and we would load up with pebbles and flints which, according to the doctor, had been fish in their time. Finally his last great passion: will-o'-the-wisps. He wanted to find a way of catching and keeping them, and with this aim in view we would spend nights wandering about our cemetery, waiting for one of those vague lights to go up among the mounds of earth and grass, when he would try to draw it towards us, make it follow us and then capture it, without its going out, in various receptacles with which we experimented: sacks, flasks, strawless demijohns, braziers, colanders. Dr. Trelawney had settled near the cemetery in a shack which had once been the gravedigger's in times of pomp and war and plague, when a man was needed on the job full-time. There the doctor had set up his laboratory, with test tubes of every shape, to bottle the wisps, and nets like those for fishing to catch them; and retorts and crucibles in which he examined the why and wherefore of those pale little flames coming from the soil of cemeteries and the exhalations of corpses. But he was not a man to remain for long absorbed in studies. He would break off and come out, and then we would go hunting together for new phenomena of nature.

I was free as air since I had no parents and belonged to the category neither of servants nor masters. I was part of the Terralba family only by tardy recognition, but did not bear their name and no one had bothered to give me any education. My poor mother had been the Viscount Aiolfo's daughter, and Medardo's elder sister, but she had besmirched the family honor by eloping with a poacher who was my father. I was born in a poacher's hut in rough undergrowth by the woods, and shortly afterward my father was killed in some squabble, and pellagra put an end to my mother who had stayed in that wretched hut all alone. Then I was brought into the castle, as my grandfather Aiolfo took pity on me, and grew up under the care of the chief nurse, Sebastiana. I remember that when Medardo was still a boy and I was a small child he would sometimes let me take part in his games as if we were of equal rank. Then distance grew between us and I dropped to the level of a servant. Now in Dr. Trelawney I found a companion such as I had never had.

The doctor was sixty but about as tall as I. He had a face lined like an old chestnut, under tricorn and wig. His legs, with gaiters halfway up his thighs, looked long and disproportionate as a cricket's, the effect being emphasized by his long strides. He wore a dove-colored tunic with red facings, and slung across it, the bottle of *cancarone* wine.

His passion for will-o'-the-wisps made him take long night marches to the cemeteries of nearby villages, where at times flames were to be seen finer in color and size than those in our abandoned cemetery. But it was bad for us if our stalking was found out by locals. Once we were mistaken for sacrilegious thieves and were followed for miles by a group of men armed with forks and tridents.

Dr. Trelawney and I hopped from rock to rock, but heard the infuriated peasants getting closer behind. At a place called Grimace's Leap was a small bridge of tree trunks straddling a deep abyss. Instead of crossing over the doctor and I hid on a ledge of rock on the abyss's very edge, just in time as the peasants were right on our heels. They did not see us, and yelling, "Where are the swine?" rushed straight at the bridge. A crack, and they were flung screaming into the torrent far below. Trelawney's and my terror for our own skins changed to relief at danger escaped and then to terror again at the awful fate that had befallen our pursuers. We scarcely dared lean over and peer down into the darkness where the peasants had vanished. Then raising our eyes we looked at the remains of the little bridge; the trunks were still firmly in place, but they were broken in half as if sawn through. That could be the only explanation for thick wood giving way with such a clean break.

"There's the hand of *you know who* in this," said Dr. Trelawney, and I understood.

Just then we heard a quick clatter of hooves and on the verge of the precipice appeared a horse and a rider half wrapped in a black cloak. It was the Viscount Medardo, who was contemplating with his frozen triangular smile the tragic success of his trap, unforeseen perhaps by himself. He must certainly have wanted to kill us two off; instead of which, as it turned out, he had saved our lives. Trembling, we saw him gallop off on that thin horse, which went leaping away over the rocks as if born of a goat.

• • •

At that time my uncle always went round on horseback. He had gotten our saddle-maker Pietrochiodo to make him a special saddle with a stirrup to which he could hitch himself, while the other had a counterweight. A sword and crutch were slung by the saddle. And so the Viscount galloped about, wearing a plumed hat with a great brim which half vanished under a wing of the ever-fluttering cloak. Wherever the sound of his horse's hooves was heard, everyone took to his heels—even more than when Galateo the leper passed—and bore off children and animals. They feared for their plants, as the Viscount's wickedness spared no one and could burst at any moment into the most unforeseen and incomprehensible actions.

He had never been ill, so never needed Dr. Trelawney's care. I don't know how the doctor would have dealt with such an eventuality as he did his very best to avoid ever hearing my uncle mentioned. When he heard people talking about the Viscount and his cruelty, Dr. Trelawney would shake his head and curl a lip with a mutter of "Oh, oh, oh . . . zzt, zzt, zzt!" It seemed that from the medical point of view my uncle's case aroused no interest in him. But I was beginning to think that he had become a doctor only from family pressure or his own convenience, and did not care a rap about the science of it. Perhaps his career as ship's doctor had been due only to his ability at card games, which made the most illustrious navigators, particularly Captain Cook himself, contend for him as partner.

One night Dr. Trelawney was fishing with a net for will-o'-the-wisps in our ancient cemetery when his eyes fell on Medardo of Terralba pasturing his horse around the tombs. The doctor was much confused and alarmed, but the Viscount came nearer and asked him in the defective pronunciation of his halved mouth, "Are you looking for night butterflies, Doctor?"

"Oh, m'lord," replied the doctor in a faint voice. "Oh, not exactly butterflies, m'lord . . . Will-o'-the-wisps, you know, will-o'-the-wisps . . ."

"Ah, will-o'-the-wisps, eh? I've often wondered about their origin too."

"They have been the subject of my modest studies for some time, m'lord . . ." said Trelawney, encouraged by his benevolent tone.

Medardo twisted his angular half face into a smile, the skin taut as a skull's. "You deserve all assistance in your studies," he said to him. "A pity that this cemetery is so abandoned, and thus no good for will-o'-the-wisps. But I promise you that I'll see about helping you as much as I can tomorrow."

Next day was the one allocated for administering justice, and the Viscount condemned a dozen peasants to death, because according to his computation they had not handed over the whole proportion of crops due from them to the castle. The dead men were buried in a common grave, and the cemetery blossomed every night with numerous will-o'-the-wisps. Dr. Trelawney was terrified by this help, useful as it was to his studies.

With all these tragic developments Master Pietrochiodo was producing greatly improved gibbets. Now they were real masterpieces of carpentry and mechanics, as were also the racks, winches and other instruments of torture by which the Viscount Medardo tore confessions from the accused. I was often in Pietrochiodo's workshop, as it was a fine sight to watch him at work with such ability and enthusiasm. But a sorrow always weighed on the saddler's heart. The scaffolds he was constructing were for innocent men. "How can I manage to get orders for work as delicate, but with a different purpose? What new mechanisms would I enjoy making more?" But finding these questions coming to no conclusions, he tried to thrust them out of his mind and settle down to making his instruments as fine and ingenious as possible.

"Just forget the purpose for which they're used," he said to me, "and look at them as pieces of mechanism. You see how fine they are?"

I looked at that architecture of beams, crisscross of ropes, links of capstans and pulleys, and tried not to see tortured bodies on them, but the more I tried the more I found myself thinking of them, and said to Pietrochiodo: "How can I forget?"

"How indeed, my lad?" replied he. "How d'you think I can, then?"

But with all their agonies and terrors, those days had times of delight. The loveliest hour was when the sun was high and the sea golden and the chickens sang as they laid their eggs and from the lane came the sound of the leper's horn. The leper would pass every morning to collect alms for his companions in misfortune. He was called Galateo, and round his neck he wore a hunting horn whose sound warned us from a distance of his arrival. Women would hear the horn and lay out eggs or melons or tomatoes and sometimes a little rabbit on the edge of the wall; and then they would run off and hide, taking their children, for no one should be out in the open when a leper goes by: leprosy can be caught from a distance and it's dangerous even to look at one. Preceded by notes on his horn, Galateo would come slowly along the deserted lanes, with a tall stick in his hand and a long tattered robe touching the ground. He had long yellow hair and a round white face already eaten away by leprosy. He gathered up the gifts, put them in his knapsack and called his thanks towards the houses of the hidden peasants in honeyed tones that always included some jolly double meaning.

In those days leprosy was very prevalent in districts near the sea, and near us was a village called Pratofungo, inhabited only by lepers, for whom we were bound to produce gifts which Galateo gathered up. When anyone from the sea or country caught leprosy, he left relatives and friends and went to Pratofungo to spend the rest of his life waiting for the disease to devour him. There were rumors of great merrymaking to greet each new arrival. From afar song and music was heard coming from the lepers' houses till nightfall.

Many things were said of Pratofungo although no healthy person had ever been there, but rumors were agreed in saying that life there was a perpetual party. Before becoming a leper colony the village had been a great place for prostitutes and visited by sailors of every race and religion; and the women there, it seemed, still kept the licentious habits of those times. The lepers did no work on the land, except for a vineyard of strawberry grapes whose juice kept them the whole year round in a state of simmering tipsiness. The lepers spent most of their time playing strange instruments of their own invention, such as harps with little bells attached to the strings, and singing in falsetto, and painting eggs with daubs of every color as if for a perpetual Easter. And so, whiling away the time with sweet music, their disfigured faces hung round with garlands of jasmine, they forgot the human community from which their disease had cut them off.

No local doctor had ever taken on the care of the lepers, but when Trelawney settled amongst us, some hoped that he might feel like dedicating his lore to healing that running sore in our locality. I shared the same hopes too, in my childish way; for some time I had been longing to get into Pratofungo and attend those lepers' parties, and had the doctor done any experimenting with his drugs on those wretches he might have allowed me to accompany him into the village sometimes. But none of this ever happened. As soon as he heard Galateo's horn Dr. Trelawney ran off at full speed and no one seemed more afraid of contagion than he. Sometimes I tried to question him on the nature of the disease, but he would make evasive or muted replies, as if the very word "leper" put him out.

Actually I can't think why we were so determined to think of him as a doctor. He was very attentive to animals, particularly small ones, or to stones or natural phenomena, but human beings and their infirmities filled him with dismay and disgust. He had a horror of blood, he would only touch the sick with the tips of his fingers, and when faced with serious cases plunged his nose in a silk bandanna dipped in vinegar. He was shy as a girl, and blushed at the sight of a naked body; if it was a woman's he would stutter and keep his eyes lowered. In all his long journeys over the oceans he never seemed to have known women. Luckily for us, in those times births were matters for midwives and not doctors, otherwise I wonder how he would have managed.

Into my uncle's head now came the notion of arson. At night all of a sudden a haystack of wretched peasants, or a tree cut for fuel, or a whole wood would burn. Then we would spend the whole night passing buckets of water from hand to hand in order to put out the flames. The victims were always poor unfortunates who had fallen out with the Viscount, either because of one of his increasingly severe and unjust orders or because of the dues he had doubled. From burning other things he then began setting fire to houses. It was thought that he came up close at night, threw burning brands on roofs and then rushed off on horseback, but no one ever managed to catch him in the act. Once two old people died. Once a boy had his brains fried. The peasants grew to hate him more and more. His most stubborn enemies were some families of Huguenots who were living in huts up on Col Gerbido. Their men kept guard all night to prevent fires.

One night without any plausible reason he even went under the houses of Pratofungo, whose roofs were thatched, and threw burning brands at them. A characteristic of lepers is to feel no pain when scorched, and had they been caught by the flames in their sleep they would never have woken again. But as the Viscount galloped away he heard a tune on a violin from the village behind him; the inhabitants of Pratofungo were still up and intent on their fun. They all got a little scorched, but felt no ill effects and amused themselves in their own way. The fire was soon put out; and their homes, perhaps because so impregnated with leprosy, suffered little damage from the flames.

Medardo's evil nature even turned him against his own

personal property, the castle itself. A fire went up in the servants' wing, and spread amid the loud shrieks of those trapped there, while the Viscount was seen galloping off into the country. It was an attempt on the life of his nurse and foster mother Sebastiana. With the stubborn bossiness that women claim over those they have seen as children, Sebastiana was constantly reproving the Viscount for his every misdeed, even when all were convinced that his nature forced him to acts of insane and irreparable cruelty. Sebastiana was pulled out from the burning walls in a very bad state and had to stay in bed for days to heal her burns.

One night the door of the room in which she was lying opened and the Viscount appeared by her bed.

"What are those marks on your face, nurse?" said Medardo, pointing at her burns.

"Marks of your sins, son," said the old woman calmly.

"Your skin is all speckled and scored. What ails you, nurse?"

"My ails are nothing, son, compared to those awaiting you in hell unless you mend your ways."

"You must get well soon; I would not like to hear of you going round with this disease on you."

"I'm not out for a husband, that I need bother about my looks. A good conscience is enough for me. I only wish you could say the same."

"And yet your bridegroom is waiting to bear you off with him, you know!"

"Do not deride old age, my son, you who have had your youth ruined."

"I do not jest. Hark, nurse; there is your bridegroom playing beneath your window . . ."

Sebastiana listened and from outside the castle heard the sound of the leper's horn.

Next day Medardo sent for Dr. Trelawney.

"Suspicious marks have appeared on the face of our old servant, I don't know how," he said to the doctor. "We're all afraid it's leprosy. Doctor, we entrust ourselves to the light of your knowledge."

Trelawney bowed and stuttered.

"M'duty, m'lord . . . at your orders, as always, m'lord . . ."

He turned, slipped out of the castle, got himself a small barrel of *cancarone* and vanished into the woods. He was not seen again for a week. When he got back Sebastiana had been sent to the leper village.

One evening at dusk she left the castle, veiled and dressed in black, with a bundle on her arm. She knew that her fate was sealed; she must take the road to Pratofungo. Leaving the room where she had been kept till then, she found the passages and stairs deserted. Down she went, across the courtyard, out into the country; all was deserted, everyone at her passage withdrew and hid. She heard a hunting horn sounding a low call on two notes only. On the path ahead of her was Galateo with the mouthpiece of his instrument raised to the sky. With slow steps the nurse advanced. The path went towards the setting sun. Galateo moved far ahead of her. Every now and then he stopped as if gazing at the bumble bees amid the leaves, raised his horn and played a sad note. The nurse looked at the flowers and banks that she was leaving, sensed behind hedges the presence of people avoiding her, and walked on. Alone, Galateo a long way behind, she reached Pratofungo, and as the village gates closed behind her harps and violins began to play.

Dr. Trelawney had disappointed me a lot. Not having moved a finger to prevent old Sebastiana from being condemned to the leper colony—though knowing that her marks were not those of leprosy—was a sign of cowardice, and for the first time I felt a sense of aversion for the doctor. On top of this he had not taken me with him when he ran off into the woods, though knowing how useful I would have been as a hunter of squirrels and finder of raspberries. Now I no longer enjoyed going with him for will-o'-the-wisps as before, and often went around alone, on the lookout for new companions.

The people who most attracted me now were the Huguenots up on Col Gerbido. They were people who had escaped from France, where the king had those who followed their religion cut into small pieces. While crossing the mountains they had lost their books and sacred objects, and now had neither Bibles to read from nor Mass to say nor hymns to sing nor prayers to recite. Suspicious, like all those who have passed through persecutions and live amid people of a different faith, they had refused to accept any religious book, or listen to any advice on how to conduct their rites. If someone came looking for them saying he was a fellow Huguenot, they suspected that he might be a Papal agent in disguise, and shut themselves off in silence. So they cultivated the harsh lands of Col Gerbido; they overworked men and women, from before dawn till after dusk, in the hope of being illuminated by Grace. Inexpert in what constituted sin, they multiplied their prohibitions lest they make mistakes, and were reduced to giving each other constant severe glances in case the least gesture betrayed a blameworthy intention. With confused memories of theological disputations, they avoided naming God or using any other religious expression, for fear of sacrilege. So they followed no rites and probably did not even dare formulate thoughts on matters of faith, though preserving an air of grave absorption as if these were constantly in their minds. But with time the rules of their agricultural labors had acquired a value equal to those of the Commandments, as had the habits of thrift and diligent housekeeping to which they were forced.

They were all one great family, with lots of grandchildren and in-laws, all tall and knobbly, and they worked the land always formally dressed in buttoned black, the men in wide-brimmed hats and the women in white kerchiefs. The men wore long beards and always went round with slung blunderbusses, but it was said that none of them had ever fired a shot, except at sparrows, as it was forbidden by the Commandments.

From chalky terraces with a few stunted vines and wretched crops would rise the voice of old Ezekiel, forever shouting with fists raised to the sky, his white goatee beard trembling, eyes rolling under his tubular hat. "Famine and plague! Famine and plague!" he would yell at his family bent over their work, "Hoe harder, Jonah! Tear at those weeds, Susanna! Spread that manure, Tobias!" and give out thousands of orders and rebukes in the bitter tone of one addressing a bunch of inept wasters. Every time, after shouting out the innumerable things they must do to prevent the land going to ruin, he would begin doing them himself, pushing away the others around, still shouting, "Famine and plague!"

His wife on the other hand never shouted, and seemed, unlike the others, secure in a secret religion of her own, which was fixed to the smallest details but never mentioned by so much as a single word to anyone. She would just stare, her eyes all pupils, and only say, through set lips, "D'you think that's right, Sister Rachel? D'you think that's right, Brother Aaron?" for the rare smiles to vanish from her family's mouths and their grave intent expressions to return.

One evening I arrived at Col Gerbido while the Huguenots were praying. Not that they pronounced any words or joined hands or knelt; they were standing in a row in the vineyard, men on one side and women on the other, with old Ezekiel at the end, his beard on his chest. They looked straight in front of them, with clenched hands hanging from long knobbly arms, but though they seemed absorbed they had not lost awareness of what was going on around them; and Tobias put out a hand and tweaked a caterpillar off a vine, Rachel crushed a snail with her nailed boot, and Ezekiel himself suddenly took off his hat to frighten sparrows on the crops.

Then they intoned a psalm. They did not remember the words, only the tune, and even that not well, and often someone went off key or maybe they all were off the whole time, but they never stopped, and on finishing one verse started another, always without pronouncing any words.

I felt a tug at my arm; it was little Esau signing me to be quiet and come with him. Esau was my age; he was old Ezekiel's last son. The only look he had of his parents was their hard, tense expression, with a sly malice of his own. We went off on all fours through the vineyard, with him saying, "They'll be at it another half hour, you see. Come and look at my lair."

Esau's lair was secret. He used to hide there so that his family could not find him and send him to look after goats or take snails off the crops. He would spend entire days there doing nothing, while his father went searching and calling for him throughout the countryside.

Esau gave me a pipe and told me to smoke it. He lit one

for himself and drew great mouthfuls with an enthusiasm I had never seen in a boy. It was the first time I had smoked; it soon made me feel sick and I stopped. To pull me together Esau drew out a bottle of *grappa* and poured me a glassful, which made me cough and wrung my guts. He drank it as if it were water.

"It takes a lot to get drunk," he said.

"Where did you find all these things you have here in your lair?" I asked him.

Esau made a gesture of clawing the air, "Stolen!"

He had put himself at the head of a band of Catholic boys who were sacking the country. They not only stripped the trees of fruit, but went into houses and hen coops. And they swore stronger and more often even than Master Pietrochiodo. They knew every swear word, Catholic and Huguenot, and exchanged them freely.

"There's a lot of other sins I commit too," he explained to me. "I bear false witness, I forget to water the beans, I don't respect father and mother, I come home late. Now I want to commit every sin there is, even the ones people say I'm not old enough to understand."

"Every sin?" I asked him. "Killing too?"

He shrugged his shoulders. "Killing's not in my line now, it's no use."

"My uncle kills and has people killed just for fun, they say," I exclaimed, just for something with which to counterbalance Esau.

Esau spat. "A thug's game," he said.

Then it thundered and outside the lair it began to rain.

"They'll be on the lookout for you at home," I said to Esau. Nobody was ever on the lookout for me, but I had seen other boys being sought by parents, particularly in bad weather, and I thought that was something important.

"Let's wait for it to stop," said Esau, "and have a game of dice."

He pulled out the dice and a heap of money. I had no money, so I gambled my whistles, knives and catapults, and lost the lot.

"Don't let it get you down," said Esau eventually. "I cheat, you know."

Outside—thunder, lightning and torrential rain. Esau's cave was flooding. He salvaged his cigars and other things and said, "It'll pour all night, better run and shelter at home."

We were soaked and muddy when we reached old Ezekiel's hut. The Huguenots were sitting around the table, illuminated by a flickering candle, and were trying to remember episodes from the Bible, taking great care to narrate them as if they had once read them.

"Famine and plague!" Ezekiel shouted, and banged a fist on the table so hard it put out the light just when his son Esau appeared in the doorway with me.

My teeth began chattering. Esau shrugged his shoulders. Outside all the thunder and lightning seemed to be unloading on Col Gerbido. As they were rekindling the light the old man with raised fists enumerated his son's sins as the foulest ever committed by any human being, but he only knew a small part of them. The mother nodded mutely, and all the other sons and sons-in-law and daughters-in-law and grandchildren listened, chins on chest and faces hidden in their hands. Esau was chewing away at an apple as if the sermon did not concern him. What with the thunder and Ezekiel's voice I was trembling like a reed.

The diatribe was interrupted by the return of the men on guard, using sacks for hoods, who were all soaking wet. The Huguenots kept guard all night long in turns, armed with muskets, scythes and pitchforks, to prevent the prowling incursions of the Viscount, now their declared enemy.

"Father! Ezekiel!" said these Huguenots. "'Tis a night for wolves. For sure the Lame One won't come. May we return home, Father?"

"Are there no signs of the Maimed One?" asked Ezekiel.

"No, Father, except for the smell of burning left by the lightning. 'Tis not a night for the Bereft One."

"Stay here and change your clothes then. May the storm bring peace to the Sideless One and to us."

The Lame One, the Maimed One, the Bereft One and the Sideless One were some of the appellations given by the Huguenots to my uncle. Never once did I hear them call him by his real name. These remarks showed a kind of intimacy with the Viscount, as if they knew a great deal about him, almost as if he were an old enemy. They would exchange brief phrases accompanied by winks and laughs.

"Ha ha! The Maimed One . . . Just like him, ha ha! The Half-Deaf One . . ." as if to them all of Medardo's dark follies were clear and foreseeable.

They were talking thus when a fist was heard knocking at the door in the storm. "Who knocks in this weather?" said Ezekiel. "Quick, open."

They opened the door and there on the threshold was the Viscount, standing on his one leg, wrapped in a dripping cloak, his plumed hat soaked with rain.

"I have tied up my horse in your stall," he said. "Will you give me hospitality too? It's a bad night for a traveler."

Everyone looked at Ezekiel. I had hidden myself beneath the table lest my uncle should discover that I frequented this enemy house.

"Sit down by the fire," said Ezekiel. "In this house a guest is always welcome."

Near the threshold was a heap of sheets, the kind used for stretching under trees to gather olives; there Medardo lay down and went to sleep.

In the dark the Huguenots gathered around Ezekiel. "Father, we have the Lame One in our hands now!" they whispered to each other. "Must we let him go? Must we let him commit other crimes against innocent folk? Ezekiel, has the hour not come for the Buttockless One to pay the price?"

The old man raised his fists to the ceiling. "Famine and plague!" he shouted, if someone can be said to shout who scarcely emits a sound but does it with all his strength. "No guest has ever been ill-treated in our house. I myself will mount guard to protect his sleep."

And with his musket ready he took his place by the sleeping Viscount. Medardo's eye opened. "What are you doing there, Master Ezekiel?"

"I protect your sleep, guest. You are hated by many."

"That I know," said the Viscount. "I do not sleep at the castle as I fear the servants might kill me as I lie."

"Nor do they love you in my house, Master Medardo. But tonight you will be respected."

The Viscount was silent for some time, and then said, "Ezekiel, I wish to be converted to your religion."

The old man said nothing.

"I am surrounded by men I do not trust," went on Medardo, "I should like to rid myself of the lot and call the Huguenots to the castle. You, Master Ezekiel, will be my minister. I will declare Terralba to be Huguenot territory and we will start a war against the Catholic princes. You and your family shall be the leaders. Are you agreed, Ezekiel? Can you convert me?"

The old man stood there straight and motionless, his big chest crossed by the bandolier of his gun. "Too many things have we forgotten in our religion," said he, "for me to dare convert anyone. I will remain in my own territory, according to my own conscience, you in yours with yours."

The Viscount raised himself on his elbow. "You know, Ezekiel, that I have not yet reported to the Inquisition the presence of heretics in my domain, and that your heads sent as a present to our bishop would at once bring me back to favor with the Curia?"

"Our heads are still on our necks, sir," said the old man. "But there is something else far more difficult to tear from us."

Medardo leapt to his foot and opened the door. "Rather would I sleep under that oak tree there than in the house of enemies." And off he hopped into the rain.

The old man called the others. "Sons, it was written that the Lame One was to come and visit us. Now he's gone; the way to our house is clear. Do not despair, sons; one day perhaps a better traveler will pass."

All the bearded Huguenots and the coiffed women bowed their heads.

"And even if no one comes," added Ezekiel's wife, "we will stay at our posts."

At that moment a streak of lightning rent the sky, and thunder made the tiles and the stones of the wall quiver. Tobias shouted, "The lightning has struck the oak tree. It is burning!"

They ran out with their lanterns and saw the great tree carbonized down through the middle, from top to roots, and the other half intact. Far off under the rain they heard a horse's hooves and by a lightning flash caught a glimpse of the cloaked figure of its thin rider.

"Father, you have saved us," said the Huguenots. "Thank you, Ezekiel."

The sky cleared to the east and it was dawn.

Esau called me aside. "You see what fools they are!" he whispered. "Look what I've done meanwhile," and he showed me a handful of glittering objects. "I took all the gold studs on the saddle while the horse was tied in the stall. You see what fools they are, not to have thought of it."

I did not like Esau's ways, and those of his relations I found oppressive. So I preferred being on my own and going to the shore to gather limpets and catch crabs. While I was on top of a little rock trying to corner a small crab, in the calm water below me I saw the reflection of a blade above my head, and fell into the sea from fright.

"Catch hold of this," said my uncle, for it was he who had come up behind me. And he tried to make me grasp his sword by the blade.

"No, I'll do it by myself," I replied, and clambered up onto a crag separated by a limb of water from the rest of the rocks.

"Are you out for crabs?" said Medardo, "I'm out for baby octopus," and he showed me his catch. They were fat baby octopuses, brown and white. Although they had been cut in two with a sword, they were still moving their tentacles.

"If only I could halve every whole thing like this," said my uncle, lying face-down on the rocks, stroking the convulsive half of an octopus, "so that everyone could escape from his obtuse and ignorant wholeness. I was whole and all things were natural and confused to me, stupid as the air; I thought I was seeing all and it was only the outside rind. If you ever become a half of yourself, and I hope you do for your own sake, my boy, you'll understand things beyond the common intelligence of brains that are whole. You'll have lost half of yourself and of the world, but the remaining half will be a thousand times deeper and more precious. And you too would find yourself wanting everything to be halved like yourself, because beauty and knowledge and justice only exists in what has been cut to shreds."

"Uh, uh!" I kept on saying, "What a lot of crabs there are here!" and I pretended to be interested only in my catch, so as to keep as far as possible from my uncle's sword. I did not return to land until he had moved off with his octopuses. But the echo of his words went on disturbing me and I could find no escape from this frenzy of his for halving. Wherever I turned, Trelawney, Pietrochiodo, the Huguenots, the lepers, we were all under the sign of the halved man, he was the master whom we served and from whom we could not succeed in freeing ourselves.

6

Hitched to the saddle of his high-jumping horse, Medardo of Terralba would be out early, up and down bluffs, leaning over precipices to gaze over a valley with the eye of a bird of prey. That is how he came to see Pamela in the middle of a field with her goats.

The Viscount said to himself, "With all my acute emotions I have nothing that corresponds to what whole people call love. If an emotion so silly is yet so important to them, then whatever may correspond in me will surely be very grand and awesome." So he decided to fall in love with Pamela, as she lay, plump and barefoot in a simple pink dress, face downwards in the grass, dozing, chatting to the goats and sniffing flowers.

But thoughts thus coldly formulated should not deceive us. At the sight of Pamela, Medardo had sensed a vague stirring of the blood, something he had not felt for ages, and he rushed into these rationalizations with a kind of alarmed haste.

On her way home at midday Pamela noticed that all the

daisies in the fields had only half their petals and the other half had been stripped off. "Dear me!" she said to herself. "Of all the girls in the valley, that this should happen to me!" For she realized that the Viscount had fallen in love with her. She picked all the halved daisies, took them home and put them among the pages of her Mass book.

That afternoon she went to the Nun's Field to pasture her ducks and let them swim in the pond. The field was covered with white parsnip blossoms, but these flowers had also suffered the fate of the daisies, as if part of each had been cut away with a snip of scissors. "Dear, oh dear me!" she said to herself. "So it's really me he wants!" And she gathered the halved parsnip blossoms in a bunch, to slip them into the frame of the mirror over her chest of drawers.

Then she put it out of her mind, tied her plaits round her head, took off her dress and had a bathe in the pond with her ducks.

That evening as she went home the fields were full of dandelion flowers. And Pamela saw that they had lost their fluff on only one side, as if someone had lain on the ground and blown just on one side, or with only half a mouth. Pamela gathered some of those halved white spheres, breathed on them and their soft fluff floated away. "Dear, oh dearie dear!" said she to herself. "He wants me, he really does. How will it all end?"

Pamela's cottage was so small that once the goats had

been let onto the first floor and the ducks onto the ground floor there was no more room. It was surrounded by bees, for the family also kept hives. The subsoil was so full of ants that a hand put down anywhere came up all black and swarming with them. Because of this Pamela's mother slept in the haystack, her father in an empty barrel and Pamela in a hammock slung between a fig and an olive tree.

On the threshold Pamela stopped. There was a dead butterfly. A wing and half the body had been crushed by a stone. Pamela let out a shriek and called her father and mother.

"Who's been here?" said Pamela.

"Our Viscount passed by a short time ago," said her father and mother. "He said he was chasing a butterfly that had stung him."

"When has a butterfly ever stung anyone?" said Pamela.

"We've been wondering too."

"The truth is," said Pamela, "that the Viscount has fallen in love with me and we must be ready for the worst."

"Uh, uh, don't get a swollen head now, don't exaggerate," answered the old couple, as old folk are apt to answer when the young don't do the same to them.

Next morning when Pamela got to the stone on which she usually sat when pasturing her goats, she let out a cry. It was all smeared with ghastly remains; half a bat and half a jellyfish, one oozing black blood and the other shiny matter, one with the wing spread and the other with soft gelatinous edges. The goat girl realized that this was a message. It meant: rendezvous on the seashore tonight. Pamela took her courage in both hands and went.

By the sea she sat on pebbles and listened to the rustle of white-flecked waves. Then came a clatter on the pebbles and Medardo galloped along the shore. He stopped, unhitched, got off his saddle.

"Pamela, I have decided to fall in love with you," he said to her.

"And is that why," she exclaimed, "you're torturing all these creatures of nature?"

"Pamela," sighed the Viscount, "we have no other language in which to express ourselves but that. Every meeting between two creatures in this world is a mutual rending. Come with me, for I have knowledge of such pain, and you'll be safer with me than with anyone else; for I do harm as do all, but the difference between me and others is that I have a steady hand."

"And will you tear me in two as you have the daisies and the jellyfish?"

"I don't know what I'll do with you. Certainly my having you will make possible certain things I never imagined. I'll take you to the castle and keep you there and no one else will ever see you and we'll have days and months to realize what we should do and we'll invent new ways of being together."

Pamela was lying on the sand and Medardo had knelt

beside her. As he spoke he waved his hand all around her, but without touching her.

"Well, first I must know what you'll do to me. You can give me a sample now and then I'll decide whether to come to the castle or not."

The Viscount slowly drew his thin bony hand near Pamela's cheek. The hand was trembling and it was not clear if it was stretched to caress or to scratch. But it had not yet touched her when he suddenly drew it back and got up.

"It's at the castle I want you," he said, hitching himself back on to his horse. "I'm going to prepare the tower you will live in. I will leave you another day to think it over, then you must make up your mind."

So saying he spurred off along the beach.

Next day Pamela climbed up the mulberry tree as usual to gather fruit, and heard a moaning and fluttering among the branches. She nearly fell off from fright. A cock was tied on a branch by its wings and was being devoured by great hairy blue caterpillars; a nest of evil insects that live on pines had settled right on the top.

This was another of the Viscount's ghastly messages, of course. Pamela's interpretation was: "Tomorrow at dawn in the wood."

With the excuse of gathering a sackful of pine cones Pamela went up into the woods, and Medardo appeared from behind a tree trunk leaning on his crutch.

"Well," he asked Pamela, "have you made up your mind to come to the castle?"

Pamela was lying stretched out on pine needles. "I've made up my mind not to go," she said, scarcely turning. "If you want me, come and meet me here in the woods."

"You'll come to the castle. The tower where you're to live is ready and you'll be its only mistress."

"You want to keep me prisoner there and then get me burnt in a fire or maybe eaten up by rats. No, no. I told you, I'll be yours if you like but here on the pine needles."

The Viscount had crouched down near her head. In his hand he had a pine needle, which he brought close on her neck and passed all round it. Pamela felt goose flesh come over her, but lay still. She saw the Viscount's face bent over her, that profile which remained a profile even when seen from the front, and that half set of teeth bared in a scissors-like smile. Medardo clutched the pine needle in his fist and broke it. He got up. "I want you shut in the castle, yes, shut in the castle!"

Pamela realized she could risk it, so she waved her bare feet in the air and said, "Here in the wood I wouldn't say no; I wouldn't do it all shut up—not if I were dead."

"I'll get you there!" said Medardo, putting his hand on the shoulder of his horse which had come up as if it were passing there by chance. He leapt on the saddle and spurred off down a forest track.

That night Pamela slept in her hammock swung between olive and fig, and in the morning, horrors! She found a little bleeding carcass in her lap. It was half a squirrel, cut as usual longways, but with its fluffy tail intact.

"Poor me!" said she to her parents. "This Viscount just won't leave me alone."

Her father and mother passed the carcass of the squirrel from hand to hand.

"But," said her father, "he's left the tail whole. That may be a good sign."

"Maybe he's beginning to be good . . ." said her mother.

"He always cuts everything in two," said her father, "but the loveliest thing on a squirrel, its tail, he respects that . . ."

"Maybe that's what the message means," exclaimed her mother. "He'll respect what's good and beautiful about you."

Pamela put her hands in her hair. "What things to hear from my own father and mother! There's something behind this; the Viscount has spoken to you . . ."

"Not spoken," said her father. "But he's let us know that he wants to visit us and will take an interest in our wretched state."

"Father, if he comes to talk to you, open up the hives and set the bees on him."

"Daughter, maybe Master Medardo is getting better . . ." said the old woman.

"Mother, if he comes to talk to you, tie him to the ant heap and leave him there."

That night the haystack where the mother slept caught fire and the barrel where the father slept came apart. In the morning the two old folk were staring at the remains when the Viscount appeared.

"I must apologize for alarming you last night," said he, "but I didn't quite know how to approach the subject. The fact is that I am attracted to your daughter Pamela and want to take her to the castle. So I wish to ask you formally to hand her over to me. Her life will change, and so will yours."

"You can imagine how pleased we'd be, my lord!" said the old man. "But if you knew what a character my daughter has! Why she told us to set the bees from the hives on you . . ."

"Think of it, my lord . . ." said the mother, "why she told us to tie you to our ant heap . . ."

Luckily Pamela came home early that day. She found her father and mother tied up and gagged, one on the beehive, the other on the ant heap. And it was lucky that the bees knew the old man and the ants had other things to do than bite the old woman. So Pamela was able to save them both.

"You see just how good the Viscount's got, eh?" said Pamela.

But the two old people were plotting something. Next day they tied up Pamela and locked her in with the animals, then they went off to the castle to tell the Viscount that if he wanted their daughter he could send down for her as they for their part were ready to hand her over.

But Pamela knew how to talk to her creatures. The ducks pecked her free from the ropes, and the goats butted down the door. Off Pamela ran, taking her favorite goat and duck. She set up house in the wood, living in a cave known only to her and to a child who brought her food and news.

That child was myself. Life was fine with Pamela in the woods. I brought her fruit, cheese and fried fish and in exchange she gave me cups of goat's milk and duck's eggs. When she bathed in pools and streams I stood guard so no one should see her.

Sometimes my uncle passed through the woods, but he kept at a distance, though showing his presence in his usual grim way. Sometimes a shower of stones would graze Pamela and her goat and duck; sometimes the trunk of a pine tree on which she was leaning gave way, undermined at its base by blows of a hatchet; sometimes a spring would be fouled by the remains of slaughtered animals.

My uncle had now taken to hunting with a crossbow, which he succeeded in maneuvering with his one arm. But he had got even grimmer and thinner, as if new agonies were gnawing at that remnant of a body of his.

One day Dr. Trelawney was going through the fields with me when the Viscount came towards us on horseback and nearly ran him down. The horse stopped with a hoof on the Englishman's chest. My uncle said, "Can you explain, Doctor; I have a feeling as if the leg I've not got were tired from a long walk. What can that mean?"

Trelawney was confused and stuttered as usual, and the Viscount spurred off. But the question must have struck the doctor, who began thinking it over, holding his head in his hands. Never had I seen him take such an interest in a case of human ills.

7

Around Pratofungo grew bushes of mint and hedges of rosemary, and it was not clear if these were wild or the paths of some herb garden. I used to wander round them breathing in the laden air and trying to find some way of reaching old Sebastiana.

Since Sebastiana had vanished along the track leading to the leper village, I remembered that I was an orphan more often. I despaired of ever getting news of her; I asked Galateo, calling out to him from the top of a tree I had climbed when he passed, but Galateo was no friend of children, who sometimes used to throw live lizards at him from treetops, and he only gave me jeering and incomprehensible replies in that treacly squeaky voice of his. Now to my curiosity to enter Pratofungo was added a yearning to see the old nurse again, and I was forever meandering around the odoriferous bushes.

Once from a tangle of thyme rose a figure in a light-colored robe and straw hat, which walked off towards the village. It was an old leper, and wanting to ask him about the nurse I got close enough for him to hear me without shouting and said, "Hey, there, sir leper!"

But at that moment, perhaps woken by my words, right by me rose another figure, who sat up and stretched. His face was all scaly like dried bark, and he had a sparse woolly white beard. He took a whistle out of his pocket and blew a jeering blast in my direction. I realized then that the sunny afternoon was full of lepers lying hidden in the bushes; now very slowly they began rising to their feet in their light-colored robes and they walked against the sun towards Pratofungo, holding musical instruments or gardening tools with which they set up a great din. I had drawn away from the bearded man, but nearly bumped right into a noseless leper combing his hair among the laurels, and however much I went jumping off through the undergrowth I kept on running into other lepers and began to realize that the only direction I could move was towards Pratofungo, whose thatched roofs stuck over with eagles' feathers were now quite close, at the foot of the slope.

Only now and again did the lepers pay me any attention, with winks of the eye and notes of the mouth organ, but I felt that the real center of that march was myself, and that they were accompanying me to Pratofungo as if I were a captured animal. The house walls in the village were painted mauve and at a window a half-dressed woman with mauve marks on face and breasts was calling out,

"The gardeners are back!" and was playing on a lyre. Other women now appeared at windows and balconies waving tambourines and singing, "Gardeners, welcome back!"

I was being very careful to keep in the middle of the lane and not touch anyone, but I found myself at a kind of crossroads, with lepers all round me, men and women, sitting out on the thresholds of their houses, dressed in faded rags and showing tumors and intimate parts, their hair stuck with hawthorn and anemone blossoms.

The lepers were holding a little concert, to all appearances in my honor. Some were bending their violins towards me with exaggerated scrapes of the bow, others made frogs' faces as soon as I looked at them, others held out strange puppets that moved up and down on strings. The concert was made up of these varying and discordant gestures and sounds, but there was a kind of jingle they kept on repeating. "Stainless was he, till he went out to blackberry."

"I'm looking for my nurse old Sebastiana," I shouted. "Can you tell me where she is?"

They burst out laughing in a knowing malicious way.

"Sebastiana!" I called, "Sebastiana! Where are you?"

"There, child," said a leper, "now be good, child," and he pointed to a door.

The door opened and out came a woman with an olive skin, maybe a Moor, half naked and tattooed with eagles' wings, who began a licentious dance. I did not quite understand what happened next; men and women flung themselves on each other and began what I afterwards realized was an orgy.

I was making myself as small as possible when suddenly through the groups appeared old Sebastiana.

"Foul swine!" she cried. "Have some regard for an innocent soul, at least."

She took me by a hand and drew me away while they went on chanting, "Stainless was he, till he went out to blackberry!"

Sebastiana was wearing a light-colored mauve robe like a nun's and already had a few marks blotching her unlined cheeks. I was happy at finding the nurse, but in despair as she had taken me by the hand and must have given me leprosy. I told her so.

"Don't worry," replied Sebastiana. "My father was a pirate and my grandfather a hermit. I know the virtues of every herb against the Moors' diseases. They sting themselves here with marjoram and mallow, but I quietly make my own decoctions from borage and watercress which prevent my getting leprosy as long as I live."

"What about those marks on your face, nurse?" asked I, much relieved but still not quite convinced.

"Greek resin. To make them think I have leprosy too. Come here now and I'll give you a drink of my piping hot tisane, for one can't take too many precautions when going about places like these."

She had taken me off to her home, a shack a little apart, clean, with washing hung out to dry; and there we talked.

"How's Medardo? How's Medardo?" she kept on asking me, and every time I spoke she interrupted with, "Ah the rascal! Ah the scoundrel! In love! Ah poor girl! And here, you can't imagine what it's like here! What they waste! To think of all the things we deprive ourselves to give Galateo, and what they do with them! That Galateo is a good-for-nothing, anyway! A bad lot, and not the only one! What they are up to at night! And by day, too! Those women! Never have I seen such shameless creatures! If they'd only mend their clothes! Filthy and ragged! Oh, I told them so to their faces . . . And d'you know their answer?"

Delighted with this visit to the nurse, off I went the next day to fish for eels. I set my line in a pool of the stream and fell asleep as I waited. I don't know how long my sleep lasted; a sound awoke me. I opened my eyes, saw a hand raised over my head, and in the hand a red hairy spider. I turned and there was my uncle in his black cloak.

I gave a start of terror, but at that moment the spider bit my uncle's hand and scuttled off. My uncle put his hand to his lips, sucked the wound a bit and said, "You were asleep and I saw a poisonous spider climbing down onto your neck from that branch. I put my hand out and it stung me."

Not a word did I believe; at least three times he had

made attempts on my life in ways like that. But that spider had certainly bitten his hand, and the hand was swelling.

"You're my nephew," said Medardo.

"Yes," I replied in slight surprise, for it was the first time he gave any sign of recognizing me.

"I recognized you at once," he said, then added, "Ah, spider! I only have one hand and you want to poison that! But better my hand than this child's neck."

I had never known my uncle to speak like that. The thought went through my mind that he was telling the truth and maybe had gone good all of a sudden, but I at once put it aside; lies and intrigue were a habit with him. Certainly he seemed much changed, with an expression that was no longer tense and cruel but languid and drawn, perhaps from fear and pain at the bite. But his clothes, dusty and oddly cut, were also different, and helped to give that impression. His black cloak was a bit tattered, with dry leaves and chestnut husks sticking to the ends; his suit too was not of the usual black velvet but of threadbare fustian, and the leg was no longer encased in a high leather boot but in a blue and white striped woolen stocking.

To show I was not curious about him I went to see if any eel had taken a bite at my line. There were no eels, but slipped over the hook was a golden ring with a diamond in it. I pulled it up and saw that the stone bore the Terralba crest.

The Viscount's eye was following me, and he said, "Don't be surprised. As I passed I saw an eel wriggling on the hook and felt so sorry for it I freed it; then thinking of the loss I'd caused the fisherman by my action, I decided to repay him with my ring, the last thing of value I possess."

I stood there open-mouthed with amazement. Medardo went on. "I didn't know at the time that the fisherman was you. Then I found you asleep on the grass and my pleasure at seeing you quickly turned to alarm at that spider coming down on you. The rest you already know." And so saying he looked sadly at his swollen purple hand.

All this might have been just a series of cruel deceptions, but I thought how lovely a sudden conversion of his feelings would be, and the joy it would also bring Sebastiana and Pamela and all the people suffering from his cruelty.

"Uncle," I said to Medardo, "wait for me here. I'll rush off to nurse Sebastiana who knows all about herbs and get her to give me one to heal spiders' bites."

"Nurse Sebastiana . . ." said the Viscount, as he lay outstretched with his hand on his chest, "How is she nowadays?"

I did not trust him enough to tell that Sebastiana had not caught leprosy and all I said was, "Oh, so so. I'm off now," and away I ran, longing more than anything else to ask Sebastiana what she thought of these strange developments.

I found the nurse still in her shack. I was panting with running and impatience, and gave her rather a confused account, but the old woman was more interested in Medardo's bite than in his acts of goodness. "A red spider, d'you say? Yes, yes, I know just the right herb . . . Once a woodsman had his arm swell up . . . He's gone good, you say? Oh well, he always was, in a way, if one knew how to take him . . . Now where did I put that herb? Just make a poultice with it . . . Yes, Medardo's always been a scatterbrain, ever since he was a child . . . Ah here's the herb, I'd put a little bag of it in reserve . . . Yes, he always was; when he got hurt he'd come and sob to his nurse . . . Is it a deep bite?"

"His left hand is all swollen up," said I.

"Oh, oh, you silly boy . . ." laughed the nurse. "The left hand . . . Where's Master Medardo's left hand? He left it behind in Bohemia with those Turks, may the devil take them, he left it there, with the whole left half of his body . . ."

"Oh yes, of course," I exclaimed. "And yet . . . he was there, I was here, he had his hand turned round like this . . . How can that be?"

"Can't you tell left from right anymore?" said the nurse. "And yet you learnt when you were five . . ."

I just couldn't make it out. Sebastiana must be right, but I remembered exactly the opposite.

"Well, take him this herb, like a good boy," said the nurse, and off I ran.

Panting hard, I reached the brook, but my uncle was no longer there. I looked around; he had vanished with that swollen, poisoned hand of his.

That evening I was wandering among the olives. And there he was, wrapped in his black mantle, standing on a bank leaning against a tree trunk. His back was turned and he was looking out over the sea. I felt fear coming over me again, and with an effort managed to say in a faint voice, "Uncle, here is the herb for the bite . . ."

The half face turned at once and contracted into a ferocious sneer.

"What herb, what bite?" he cried.

"The herb to heal . . ." I said. But the sweet expression of before had vanished, it must have been but a passing moment's; perhaps it was slowly returning now in a tense smile, but that was obviously put on.

"Ah yes . . . fine . . . Put it in the hollow of that tree trunk . . . I'll take it later then," he said.

I obeyed and put my hand in the hollow. It was a wasps' nest. They all flew at me. I began to run, followed by the swarm, and flung myself into the stream. By swimming underwater I managed to put the wasps off my track. Raising my head I heard the Viscount's grim laugh in the distance.

Another time too he managed to deceive me. But there were many things I did not understand, and I went to Dr. Trelawney to talk to him about them. In his sexton's hut, by the light of a lantern, the Englishman was crouched over a book of human anatomy, very rare for him.

"Doctor," I asked him, "have you ever heard of a man bitten by a red spider coming through unharmed?"

"A red spider, did you say?" The doctor started. "Who had another bite from a red spider?"

"My uncle the Viscount," I said. "And I'd brought him an herb from Sebastiana, and from being good, as it seemed before, he became bad again and refused my help."

"I have just tended the Viscount for a red spider's bite on his hand," said Trelawney.

"Tell me, Doctor, did you find him good or bad?"

Then the doctor described to me what had happened.

After I left the Viscount sprawled on the grass with his swollen hand Dr. Trelawney had passed that way. He noticed the Viscount and, seized with fear as always, tried to hide among the trees. But Medardo had heard his footsteps and got up and called, "Who's there?"

The Englishman thought, "If he finds it's me hiding from him there's no knowing what he won't do," and ran off so as not to be recognized. But he stumbled and fell into a pool in the stream. Although he had spent his life on ships, Dr. Trelawney did not know how to swim, and was threshing about in the middle of the pool shouting for help. Then the Viscount said, "Wait for me," went on to the bank and got into the water, swung by his aching hand on an extended tree root, and stretched out until his foot could be seized by the doctor. Long and thin as he was, he acted as a rope for the doctor to reach the bank.

There they are, both safe and sound, with the doctor stuttering, "Oh oh, m'lord . . . thank you indeed, m'lord . . . How can I? . . ." and he sneezes right in the other's face, as he'd caught a cold.

"Good luck!" says Medardo. "But cover yourself, please," and he puts his cloak over the doctor's shoulders.

The doctor protests, more confused than ever. And the Viscount exclaims, "Keep it, it's yours."

Then Trelawney notices Medardo's swollen hand.

"What bit you?"

"A red spider."

"Let me tend it, m'lord."

And he takes him to his sexton's hut, where he does up the hand with medicines and bandages. Meanwhile the Viscount chats away with him, all humanity and courtesy. They part with a promise to see each other soon and reinforce their friendship.

"Doctor!" I said after listening to his tale. "The Viscount whom you tended shortly afterwards went back to his cruel madness and roused a whole nest of wasps against me."

"Not the one I tended," said the doctor with a wink.

"What d'you mean, Doctor?"

"I'll tell you later. Now not a word to anyone. And leave me to my studies, as there are difficult times ahead."

And Dr. Trelawney took no more notice of me; back he went to that unusual reading of a treatise on human anatomy. He must have had some plan or other in his head, and for all the following days remained reticent and absorbed.

• • •

Now news of Medardo's double nature began coming from various sources. Children lost in the woods were approached to their terror by the half man with a crutch who led them home by the hand and gave them figs and flowers and sweets; poor widows were helped across brooks by him; dogs bitten by snakes were tended, mysterious gifts were found on thresholds and windowsills of the poor, fruit trees torn up by the wind were straightened and put back into their sockets before their owners had put a nose outside the door.

At the same time, though, appearances of the Viscount half wrapped in his black cloak were also a signal for dire events; children were kidnapped and later found imprisoned in caves blocked by stones; branches broke off and rocks rolled onto old women; newly ripe pumpkins were slashed to pieces from wanton malice.

For some time the Viscount's crossbow had been used only against swallows and in such a way as not to kill but only wound and stun them, but now they were seen in the sky with legs bandaged and tied to splints, or with wings stuck together or waxed. A whole swarm of swallows so treated were prudently flying about together, like convalescents from a bird hospital, and there was an incredible rumor that Medardo was their doctor.

Once a storm caught Pamela, together with her goat and duck, in a wild and distant spot. She knew that nearby was a cave, very small, a kind of hollow in the rock, and she went towards it. Sticking out of it she saw a tattered and patched boot. Inside was huddling the half body wrapped in its black cloak. She was just going to run away, but the Viscount had already seen her, came out under the pouring rain and said to her, "Come, girl, take refuge here."

"No, I'm not taking any refuge there," said Pamela, "as there's scarcely room for one and you want to squeeze up to me."

"Don't be alarmed," said the Viscount. "I will stay outside and you take ease in there, with your goat and your duck too."

"The goat and duck can get wet."

"They'll take refuge too, you'll see."

Pamela, who had heard tell of strange impulses of goodness by the Viscount, said to herself, "We'll just see," and crouched down inside the cave, tight against her goat and duck. The Viscount stood up in front and held his cloak there like a tent so that neither she nor goat nor duck got wet. Pamela looked at the hand holding the cloak, remained for a moment deep in thought, began looking at her own hands, compared them to each other, then burst into a roar of laughter.

"I'm glad to see you so jolly, girl," said the Viscount. "But why are you laughing, if I may ask?"

"I'm laughing because I've understood what is driving all my fellow villagers quite mad."

"What is that?"

"That you are in part good and in part bad. Now it's all obvious."

"Why's that?"

"Because I've realized that you are the other half. The Viscount living in the castle, the bad one, is one half. And you're the other, who was thought lost in the war but has now returned. And it's a good half."

"That's nice of you. Thank you."

"Oh, it's the truth, not a compliment."

Now this was Medardo's story, as Pamela heard it that evening. It was not true that the cannon ball had blown part of his body to bits; it had split him in two halves. One was found by the army stretcher bearers, the other remained buried under a pyramid of Christian and Turkish corpses and was not seen. Deep in the night through the battlefield passed two hermits, whether faithful to the true religion or necromancers is not certain. They, as happens to some in wars, had been reduced to living in the no man's land between battlefields, and maybe, according to some nowadays, were trying to embrace at the same time the Christian Trinity and the Allah of Mahomet. In their peculiar piety these hermits, on finding Medardo's halved body, had taken him to their den, and there, with balsams and unguents prepared by themselves, tended and saved him. As soon as his strength was reestablished the wounded man bade farewell to his saviors and, supported on his crutch, moved for months and years throughout all the nations of Christendom in order to return to his castle, amazing people along the way by his acts of goodness.

After having told Pamela his story, the good half of the Viscount asked the shepherd girl to tell him hers. Pamela explained how the bad Medardo was laying siege to her and how she had fled from home and was now wandering in the woods. At Pamela's account the good Medardo was moved, his pity divided between the goat girl's persecuted virtue, the bad Medardo's hopeless desolation, and the solitude of Pamela's poor parents.

"As for them," said Pamela, "my parents are just a pair of old rogues. There's no point in your pitying them."

"Oh, but just think of them, Pamela, how sad they'll be in their old home at this hour, without anyone to look after them and work the fields and do out the stall."

"It can fall on their heads can the stall, for all I care!" said Pamela. "I'm beginning to realize that you're a bit too soft, and instead of attacking that other half of yours for all the swinish things he does, you seem almost to pity him as well."

"Of course I do! I know what it means to be half a man, and of course I pity him."

"But you're different; you're a bit daft too, but good."

Then the good Medardo said, "Oh, Pamela, that's the good thing about being halved. One understands the sorrow of every person and thing in the world at its own incompleteness. I was whole and did not understand, and moved about deaf and unfeeling amid the pain and sorrow all round us, in places where as a whole person one would least think to find it. It's not only me, Pamela, who am a split being, but you and everyone else too. Now I have a fellowship which I did not understand, did not know before, when whole, a fellowship with all the mutilated and incomplete things in the world. If you come with me, Pamela, you'll learn to suffer with everyone's ills, and tend your own by tending theirs."

"That all sounds very fine," said Pamela, "but I'm in a great pickle with that other part of you being in love with me and my not knowing what he wants to do with me."

My uncle let his cloak fall, as the storm was over.

"I'm in love with you too, Pamela."

Pamela jumped out of the cave. "What fun! There's the sign of the whale in the sky and I've a new lover! This one's halved too, but has a good heart."

They were walking under branches still dripping, through paths all mud. The Viscount's half mouth was curved in a sweet, incomplete smile.

"Well, what shall we do?" said Pamela.

"I'd say you ought to go back to your parents, poor things, and help them a bit in their work."

"You go if you want to," said Pamela.

"I do indeed want to, my dear," exclaimed the Viscount.

"I'll stay here," said Pamela, and stopped with her duck and goat.

"Doing good together is the only way to love."

"A pity. I thought there were other ways."

"Good-bye, my dear. I'll bring you some honey cake." And he hopped off on his stick along the path.

"What d'you say, goatee? What d'you say, duckling dear?" exclaimed Pamela when alone with her pets. "Why must all these oddities happen to *me*?"

8

When the news got around that the Viscount's other half had reappeared, things at Terralba became very different.

In the morning I accompanied Dr. Trelawney on his round of visits to the sick; for the doctor was gradually returning to the practice of medicine and was realizing how many ills our people suffered, their fiber undermined by the long famines of recent times—ills which he had not bothered about before.

We would go around the country lanes and find the signs of my uncle having preceded us. My good uncle, I mean, the one who every morning not only went the rounds of the sick, but also of the poor, the old, or whoever needed help.

In Bacciccia's orchard the ripe pomegranates were each tied round with a piece of rag. From this we understood that Bacciccia had a toothache. My uncle had wrapped up the pomegranates lest they fall off and be squashed, now that their owner's ills were preventing him from coming out and picking them himself; but it was also a signal for Dr. Trelawney to pay the sick man a visit and bring his pincers.

Prior Cecco had a sunflower on his terrace in starved soil so that it never flowered. One morning we found three chickens tied on the railing there, all pecking grain as fast as they could and unloading their white excrement in the sunflower pot. We realized that the prior must have diarrhea. My uncle had tied up the chickens there to manure the sunflower, and also to warn Dr. Trelawney of this urgent case.

On old Giromina's steps we saw a row of snails moving up towards the door; they were big snails of the kind that are eaten cooked. This was a present from the woods brought by my uncle to Giromina, but also a sign that the old woman's heart disease had got worse and that the doctor should enter quietly lest he give her a fright.

All these methods of communication were used by the good Medardo so as not to alarm the sick by too brusque a request for the doctor's help, but also so that Trelawney should get some notion of the case to be treated before entering, and thus overcome his reluctance to set foot in the houses of others and to approach sick whose ills he did not know.

Suddenly throughout the valley ran the alarm, "The Bad 'Un! The Bad 'Un's coming."

It was my uncle's bad half who had been seen riding

in the neighborhood. Then everyone ran to hide, Dr. Trelawney first, with me behind.

We passed by Giromina's, and on the steps was a streak of cracked snails, all slime and bits of shell.

"He's passed this way! Quick!"

On Prior Cecco's terrace the chickens were tied to the pan where tomatoes had been laid out to dry, and were ruining the lot.

"Quick!"

In Bacciccia's orchard the pomegranates had all been squashed on the ground and empty rag ends hung from the branches.

"Quick!"

So we spent our lives between doing good and being frightened. The Good 'Un (as my uncle's left half was called in contrast to the Bad 'Un who was the other) was now considered a saint. The maimed, the poor, the women betrayed, all those with troubles went to him. He could have profited by this to become Viscount himself. Instead of which he went on being a vagabond, going round half wrapped in his ragged black cloak, leaning on his crutch, his blue and white stocking full of holes, doing good both to those who asked him and to those who thrust him harshly from their doors. No sheep that broke a leg in a ravine, no drunk drawing a knife in a tavern, no adulterous wife hurrying to her lover by night but found him appearing as if dropped from the sky, black and thin and sweetly smiling, to help and advise, to prevent violence and sin.

Pamela was still in the woods. She had made herself a swing between two pine trees, then another firmer one for the goat and a lighter one for the duck, and she spent the hours swinging herself to and fro with her pets. But at fixed times the Good 'Un would come hobbling through the pine trees, with a bundle tied to his shoulder. It held clothes to be washed and mended which he had gathered from lonely beggars, orphans and sick; and he got Pamela to wash them, thus giving her a chance to do good too. Pamela, who was getting bored with always being in the woods, washed the clothes in the brook and he helped her. Then she hung them all to dry on the ropes of her swings, while the Good 'Un sat on a stone and read Tasso's "Jerusalem Liberated."

Pamela took no notice of the reading and lay on the grass taking it easy, delousing herself (for while living in the woods she had got a few on her), scratching herself with a plant whose literal name was "bum scratch," yawning, dangling stones in her bare toes, and looking at her legs, which were pink and plump as ever. The Good 'Un, without ever raising his eyes from the book, would go on declaiming octave after octave, with the aim of civilizing the rustic girl's manners.

But she, unable to follow the thread, and bored, was quietly inciting the goat to lick the Good 'Un's half face and the duck to perch on the book. The Good 'Un started back and raised the book, which closed. At that very moment the Bad 'Un appeared at a gallop among the trees, brandishing a great scythe against the Good 'Un. The scythe's blade fell on the book and cut it neatly in half lengthways. The back part remained in the Good 'Un's hand, and the rest fluttered through the air in a thousand half pages. The Bad 'Un vanished at a gallop; he had certainly tried to scythe the Good 'Un's half-head off, but the goat and duck had appeared just at the right moment. Pages of Tasso with their white margins and halved verses flew about in the wind and came to rest on pine branches, on grass, on water in the brook. From the top of a hillock Pamela looked at the white flutter and cried, "How lovely!"

A few leaves reached a path along which Dr. Trelawney and I were passing. The doctor caught one in the air, turned it over and over, tried to decipher those verses with no head or tail to them and shook his head. "But I can't understand a thing . . . tst . . . tst . . ."

The Good 'Un's reputation even reached the Huguenots, and old Ezekiel was often seen standing on the highest terrace of yellow vineyard, gazing at the stony mule path up from the valley.

"Father," one of his sons said to him, "I see you are looking down into the valley as if awaiting someone's arrival."

"'Tis man's lot to wait," replied Ezekiel, "and the just man's to wait with trust, the unjust man's with fear."

"Is it the Lame-One-on-the-other-foot that you are waiting for?"

"Have you heard him spoken of?"

"There's nothing else but the Half Man spoken of down in the valley. Do you think he will come up to us here?"

"If ours is the land of those who live in the right, and he is one who lives in the right, there is no reason why he should not come."

"The mule path is steep for one who has to do it on a crutch."

"There was a one-footed man who found himself a horse with which to come up."

Hearing Ezekiel talk, the other Huguenots had appeared from among the vines and gathered around him. And hearing an allusion to the Viscount they quivered silently.

"Father Ezekiel," they said, "that night when the Thin One came and the lightning burnt half the oak tree, you said that maybe one day we would be visited by a better traveler."

Ezekiel nodded and lowered his beard to his chest.

"Father, the one talked of now is as much a cripple as the other, his opposite in both body and soul, kind as the other was cruel. Could he be the visitor whom your words announced?"

"It could be every traveler on every road," said Ezekiel, "and so he, too."

"Then let's all hope that it be he!" said the Huguenots.

Ezekiel's wife came forward with her eyes fixed before her, pushing a wheelbarrow full of vine twigs. "We always hope for everything good," said she, "but even if he who hobbles over these hills is but some poor soldier mutilated in the war, good or bad in soul, we must continue every day to do right and to cultivate our land."

"That is understood," replied the Huguenots. "Have we indeed said anything that meant the contrary?"

"Then, if we are all agreed," said the woman, "we can go back to our hoes and pitchforks."

"Plague and famine!" burst out Ezekiel. "Who told you to stop work, anyway?"

The Huguenots scattered among the vine rows to reach their tools left in the furrows, but at that moment Esau, who since his father was not looking had climbed up the fig tree to eat the early fruit, cried, "Down there! Who's arriving on that mule?"

A mule was in fact coming up the slope with half a man tied to the crupper. It was the Good 'Un, who had bought an old nag when they were just about to drown her in the stream as she was so far gone it was not worth sending her to the slaughterhouse.

"Anyway I'm only half a man's weight," he said to himself, "and the old mule might still bear me. And with my own mount I can go further and do more good." So his first journey was up to pay a visit to the Huguenots.

The Huguenots greeted him all lined up, standing stiffly to attention, singing a psalm. Then the old man went up to him and greeted him like a brother. The Good 'Un dismounted and answered these greetings ceremoniously, kissed the hand of Ezekiel's wife as she stood there grim and frowning, asked after everyone's health, put out his hand to stroke the tousled head of Esau, who drew back, interested himself in everyone's trouble, made them tell the story of their persecutions and was touched. They talked, of course, without dwelling on religious controversy, as if it were a sequence of misfortunes imputable to the general wickedness of man. Medardo passed over the fact that the persecutions were by the Church to which he belonged, and the Huguenots on their part did not launch out on any affirmations of faith, partly also for fear of saying things that were theologically mistaken. So they ended up by making vague charitable speeches, disapproving of all violence and excess. All were agreed, but it was a bit chilling on the whole.

Then the Good 'Un visited the fields, commiserated with them on the bad crops, and was pleased to hear that if nothing else they had a good crop of rye.

"How much d'you sell it for?" he asked.

"Three *scudi* the pound," said Ezekiel.

"Three *scudi* the pound? But the poor of Terralba are dying of hunger, my friends, and cannot buy even a handful of rye! Perhaps you don't know that hail has destroyed the rye crop in the valley, and you are the only ones who can preserve many families from famine?"

"We do know that," said Ezekiel. "And this is just why we can sell our rye well . . ."

"But think of the help it would be for those poor people if you lowered the price . . . Think of the good you can do . . ."

Old Ezekiel stopped in front of the Good 'Un with arms crossed, and all the Huguenots imitated him.

"To do good, brother," he said, "does not mean lowering our prices."

The Good 'Un went over the fields and saw aged Huguenots like skeletons working the soil in the sun.

"You have a bad color," he said to an old man who had such a long beard he was hoeing it into the ground. "Don't you feel well?"

"Well as someone can feel who hoes for ten hours a day at the age of seventy with only thin soup in his belly."

"'Tis my cousin Adam," said Ezekiel, "an exceptional worker."

"At your age you must rest and nourish yourself," the Good 'Un was just saying, but Ezekiel dragged him brusquely away.

"All of us here earn our bread the hard way, brother," said he in a tone that admitted of no reply.

When he first got off his mule the Good 'Un had insisted on tying it up himself, and asked for a sack of fodder to refresh it after the climb. Ezekiel and his wife had looked at each other, as according to them a mule like that needed only a handful of wild chicory, but it was at the warmest moment of greeting the guest, and they had the fodder brought. Now though, thinking it over, old Ezekiel felt he really could not let that old carcass of a mule eat up the little fodder they had, and out of his guest's earshot he called Esau and said, "Esau, go quietly up to the mule, take the fodder away, and give it something else."

"A decoction for asthma?"

"Maize husks, chickpea covers, what you like."

Off went Esau, took the sack from the mule and got a kick which made him walk lame for a time. To make up for this he hid the remaining fodder to sell on his own account, and said that the mule had finished the lot.

It was dusk. The Good 'Un was in the middle of the fields with the Huguenots and they no longer knew what to say to each other.

"We still have a good hour of work ahead of us, guest," said Ezekiel's wife.

"Well then, I'll leave you."

"Good luck to you, guest."

And back the good Medardo went on his mule.

"A poor creature, mutilated in the wars," said the woman

when he had gone. "What a number there are round here! Poor wretches!"

"Poor wretches indeed," agreed the whole family.

"Plague and famine!" old Ezekiel was shouting as he went over the fields, fists raised at botched work and damage from drought. "Plague and famine!"

9

Often in the mornings I used to go to Pietrochiodo's workshop to see the ingenious carpenter's constructions. He lived in growing anguish and remorse, since the Good 'Un had been visiting him at night, reproving him for the tragic purpose of his inventions, and inciting him to produce mechanisms set in motion by good men and not by an evil urge to torture.

"What machine should I make then, Master Medardo?" asked Pietrochiodo.

"I'll tell you. For example you can . . ." and the Good 'Un began to describe a machine which he would have ordered were he the Viscount instead of his other half, and to help out his explanation he traced some confused designs.

Pietrochiodo thought at first that this machine must be an organ, a huge organ whose keys would produce sweet music, and was about to look for suitable wood for the pipes when from another conversation with the Good 'Un he got his ideas more confused, as it seemed that Medardo wanted not air but wheat to pass through the pipes! In fact it was to be not only an organ but a mill grinding corn for the poor, and also possibly an oven for baking. Every day the Good 'Un improved his idea and covered more and more paper with plans, but Pietrochiodo could not manage to keep up with him; for this organ-cum-mill-cum-bakery was also to draw up water from wells, so saving donkeys' work, and was to move about on wheels for serving different villages, while on holidays it was to hang suspended in the air with nets all round, catching butterflies.

The carpenter was beginning to doubt whether building good machines was not beyond human possibility when the only ones which could function really practically and exactly seemed to be gibbets and racks. In fact as soon as the Bad 'Un explained to Pietrochiodo an idea for a new mechanism, the carpenter found a way of doing it occurring to him immediately; and he would set to work and would find every detail coming out perfect and irreplaceable, and the instrument when finished a masterpiece of ingenious technique.

The torturing thought came to the carpenter, "Can it be in my soul, this evil which makes only my cruel machines work?" But he went on inventing other tortures with great zeal and ability.

One day I saw him working on a strange instrument of execution, with a white gibbet framed in a wall of black wood, and a rope, also white, running through two holes in the wall at the exact place of the noose.

"What is that machine, Master?" I asked him.

"A gibbet for hanging in profile," he said.

"Who have you built it for?"

"For one man who both condemns and is condemned. With half of his head he condemns himself to capital punishment, and with the other half he enters the noose and breathes his last. I want to arrange it so one can't tell which is which."

I realized that the Bad 'Un, feeling the popularity of his good half growing, had arranged to get rid of him as soon as possible.

In fact he called his constables and said, "For far too long a low vagabond has been infesting our estates and sowing discord. By tomorrow the criminal must be captured and brought here to die."

"Lordship, it will be done," said the constable, and off they went. Being one-eyed, the Bad 'Un had not noticed that when answering him they had winked at each other.

For it should be told that a palace plot had been hatching in those days and the constabulary were part of it too. The aim was to imprison and suppress the reigning half-Viscount and hand castle and title over to the other half. The latter however knew nothing of this. And that night he woke up in the hayloft where he lived and found himself surrounded by constables.

"Have no fear," said the head constable. "The Viscount has sent us to murder you, but we are weary of his cruel tyranny and have decided to murder him and put you in his place."

"What do I hear? Has this been done? I ask you. The Viscount, you have not already murdered him, have you?"

"No, but we surely will in the course of the morning."

"Thanks be to Heaven! No, do not stain yourself with more blood, too much has been shed already. What good could come of rule born of crime?"

"No matter, we'll lock him in the tower and not bother any more about him."

"Do not raise your hands against him or anyone else, I beg you! I too am pained by the Viscount's arrogance; yet the only remedy is to give him a good example, by showing ourselves kind and virtuous."

"Then we'll have to murder you, Signore."

"Ah no! I told you not to murder anyone."

"What can we do then? If we don't suppress the Viscount we must obey him."

"Take this phial. It contains a few drops, the last that remain to me, of the unguent with which the Bohemian hermits healed me and which till now has been most precious to me at a change of weather, when my great scar hurts. Take it to the Viscount and say merely, 'Here is a gift from one who knows what it means to have veins that end in plugs!'"

The constables took the phial to the Viscount, who condemned them to be hanged. To save the constables the other plotters planned a rising. They were clumsy, and let out news of the revolt, which was suppressed in blood. The

Good 'Un took flowers to the graves and consoled widows and orphans.

Old Sebastiana was never moved by the goodness of the Good 'Un. When about his zealous enterprises, the Good 'Un would often stop at the old nurse's shack and visit her, always full of kindness and consideration. And every time she would preach him a sermon. Perhaps because of her maternal instinct, perhaps because old age was beginning to cloud her mind, the nurse took little account of Medardo's separation into two halves. She would criticize one half for the misdeeds of the other, give one advice which only the other could follow and so on.

"Why did you cut off the head of old Granny Bigin's chicken, poor old woman, which was all she had? You're too grown-up now to do such things . . ."

"Why d'you say that to me, nurse? You know it wasn't me . . ."

"Oho! Then just tell me who it was?"

"Me but—"

"There, you see!"

"But not me here . . ."

"Ah, because I'm old you think I'm soft too, do you? When I hear people talk of some rascality I can tell at once if it's one of yours. And I say to myself, I swear Medardo's hand is in that . . ."

"But you're always mistaken . . ."

"I'm mistaken, am I! You young people tell us old folk that we're mistaken . . . And what about you? You went and gave your crutch to old Isodoro . . ."

"Yes, that was me . . ."

"D'you boast of it? He used it for beating his wife, poor woman . . ."

"He told me he couldn't walk because of gout . . ."

"He was pretending . . . And you at once go and give him your crutch . . . Now he's broken it on his wife's back and you go round on a twisted branch . . . You've no head, that's what's the matter with you! Always like this! And what about that time when you made Bernardo's bull drunk with *grappa* . . ."

"That wasn't . . ."

"Oho, so it wasn't you! That's what everyone says, but it's always him, the Viscount!"

The Good 'Un's frequent visits to Pratofungo were due, apart from his filial attachment to the nurse, to the fact that he was then dedicating himself to helping the poor lepers. Immune from contagion (also due, apparently to the mysterious cures of the hermits) he would wander about the village informing himself minutely of each one's needs, and not leave them in peace until he had done every conceivable thing he could for them. Often he would go to and fro on his mule between Pratofungo and Dr. Trelawney's, for advice and medicines. The doctor himself had not the courage to go near the lepers, but he seemed, with the good Medardo as intermediary, to be beginning to take an interest in them.

But my uncle's intentions went further. He was proposing to tend not only the bodies of the lepers but their souls too. And he was forever among them, moralizing away, putting his nose into their affairs, being scandalized, and preaching. The lepers could not endure him. Pratofungo's happy licentious days were over. With this thin figure on his one leg, black-dressed, ceremonious and sententious, no one could have fun without arousing public recriminations, malice and backbiting. Even their music, by dint of being criticized as futile, lascivious and inspired by evil sentiments, grew burdensome and those strange instruments of theirs got covered with dust. The leper women, deprived of their revels, suddenly found themselves face to face with their disease and spent their evenings sobbing in despair.

"Of the two halves the Good 'Un is worse than the Bad 'Un," they began to say at Pratofungo.

But it was not only among the lepers that admiration for the Good 'Un was decreasing.

"Lucky that cannon ball only split him in two," everyone was saying. "If it had done it in three, who knows what we'd have to put up with!"

The Huguenots now kept guard in turns to protect themselves from him too, as he had now lost respect for them, and would come up at all hours spying out how many sacks were in their granaries, and preaching to them about their prices being too high and spreading this around, so ruining their business.

Thus the days went by at Terralba, and our sensibilities became numbed, since we felt ourselves lost between an evil and a virtue equally inhuman.

10

There is never a moonlight night but wicked ideas in evil souls writhe like serpents in nests, and charitable ones sprout lilies of renunciation and dedication. So Medardo's two halves wandered, tormented by opposing furies, amid the crags of Terralba.

Then each came to a decision on his own, and next morning set out to put it into practice.

Pamela's mother was just about to draw water when she stumbled into a snare and fell into the well. She hung on a rope and shrieked "Help!" Then, in the circle of the wellhead, against the sky she saw the silhouette of the Bad 'Un, who said to her, "I just wanted to talk to you. This is what I've decided. Your daughter Pamela is often seen about with a halved vagabond. You must make him marry her. He has compromised her now and if he's a gentleman he must put it right. That's my decision: don't ask me to explain more."

Pamela's father was taking a sack of olives from his

grove to the oil press, but the sack had a hole in it, and a dribble of olives followed him along the path. Feeling his burden grown lighter, the old man took the sack from his shoulders and realized it was almost empty. But behind him he saw the Good 'Un gathering up the olives one by one and putting them in his cloak.

"I was following you in order to have a word and had the good fortune of saving your olives. This is what is in my heart. For some time I have been thinking that the unhappiness of others which I desire to help is perhaps increased by my very presence. I intend to leave Terralba. But I do so only if my departure will give peace back to two people — to your daughter who sleeps in a cave while a noble destiny awaits her, to my unhappy right part who should not be left so lonely. Pamela and the Viscount must be united in matrimony."

Pamela was training a squirrel when she met her mother, who was pretending to look for pine cones.

"Pamela," said her mother, "the time has come for that vagabond called the Good 'Un to marry you."

"Where does that idea come from?" said Pamela.

"He has compromised you and he shall marry you. He's so kind that if you tell him so he won't say no."

"But how did you get such an idea in your head?"

"Quiet! If you knew who told me you wouldn't ask so many questions; it was the Bad 'Un in person told me, our most illustrious Viscount!"

"Oh dear!" said Pamela, dropping the squirrel in her lap. "I wonder what trap he's preparing for us."

Soon afterwards she was teaching herself to hum through a blade of grass when she met her father, who was pretending to look for wood.

"Pamela," said her father, "it's time you said 'yes' to the Viscount, the Bad 'Un, on condition you marry in church."

"Is that your idea or someone else's?"

"Wouldn't you like to be a Viscountess?"

"Answer my question."

"All right; imagine, it was told me by the best-hearted man in all the world, the vagabond they call the Good 'Un."

"Oh, that one has nothing else to think of. You wait and see what I arrange!"

Ambling through the thickets on his gaunt horse, the Bad 'Un thought over his stratagem; if Pamela married the Good 'Un then by law she would be wife to Medardo of Terralba, his wife that is. By this right the Bad 'Un would easily be able to take her from his rival, so meek and unaggressive.

Then he met Pamela, who said to him, "Viscount, I have decided that we'll marry if you are willing."

"You and who?" exclaimed the Viscount.

"Me and you, and I'll come to the castle and be the Viscountess."

The Bad 'Un had not expected this at all, and thought, "Then it's useless to arrange all the play-acting of getting her married to my other half; I'll marry her myself and that'll be that."

So he said, "Right."

Pamela said, "Arrange things with my father."

A little later Pamela met the Good 'Un on his mule.

"Medardo," she said, "I realize now that I'm really in love with you and if you wish to make me happy you must ask for my hand in marriage."

The poor man, who had made that great renunciation for love of her, sat open-mouthed. "If she's happy to marry me, I can't get her to marry the other one any more," he thought, and said, "My dear, I'll hurry off to see about the ceremony."

"Arrange things with my mother, do," said she.

All Terralba was in a ferment when it was known that Pamela was to marry. Some said she was marrying one, some the other. Her parents seemed to be trying to confuse ideas on purpose. Up at the castle everything was certainly being polished and decorated for a great occasion. And the Viscount had made a suit of black velvet with a big puff on the sleeve and another on the thigh.

But the vagabond had also had his poor mule brushed up and mended his clothes at elbow and knee. In church all the candelabras were aglitter.

Pamela said that she would not leave the wood until the moment of the nuptial procession. I did the commissions for her trousseau. She sewed herself a white dress with a veil and a long train and made up a circlet and belt of lavender sprigs. As she still had a few yards of veil left, she made a wedding robe for the goat and a wedding dress for the duck, and so ran through the woods, followed by her two pets, until the veil got all torn in the branches and her train gathered every pine cone and chestnut husk drying along the paths.

But the night before the wedding she was thoughtful and a bit alarmed. Sitting at the top of a hillock bare of trees, with her train wrapped round her feet, her lavender circlet all awry, she propped her chin on her hand and looked round sighing at the woods.

I was always with her, for I was to act as page, together with Esau, who was, however, not to be found.

"Who will you marry, Pamela?" I asked her.

"I don't know," she said. "I really don't know what might happen. Will it go well? Will it go badly?"

Every now and again from the woods rose a kind of guttural cry or a sigh. It was the two halved swains who, prey to the excitement of the vigil, were wandering through glades in the woods, wrapped in their black cloaks, one on his bony horse, the other on his bald mule, moaning and sighing in anxious imaginings. And the horse leaped over ledges and landslides, and the mule clambered over slopes and hillsides, without their two riders ever meeting.

Then at dawn the horse, urged to a gallop, was lamed in a ravine; and the Bad 'Un could not get to the wedding in time. The mule on the other hand went slowly and carefully and the Good 'Un reached the church punctually, just as the bride arrived with her train held by me and by Esau, who had finally been dragged down.

The crowd was a bit disappointed at seeing that the only bridegroom to arrive was the Good 'Un leaning on his crutch. But the marriage was duly celebrated, the bride and groom said yes and the ring was passed and the priest said, "Medardo of Terralba and Pamela Marcolfi, I hereby join you in holy matrimony."

Just then from the end of the nave, supporting himself on his crutch, entered the Viscount, his new velvet suit slashed, dripping and torn. And he said, "I am Medardo of Terralba and Pamela is my wife."

The Good 'Un staggered up face to face with him. "I am the Medardo whom Pamela has married."

The Bad 'Un flung away his crutch and put his hand to his sword. The Good 'Un had no option but do the same.

"On guard!"

The Bad 'Un threw himself into a lunge, the Good 'Un went into defense, but both of them were soon rolling on the floor.

They agreed that it was impossible to fight balanced on one leg. The duel must be put off to be better prepared.

"D'you know what I'll do?" said Pamela. "I'm going back to the woods." And away she ran from the church, with no pages any longer holding her train. On the bridge she found the goat and duck waiting, and they trotted along beside her.

The duel was fixed for dawn next day in the Nun's Field. Master Pietrochiodo invented a kind of leg in the shape of a compass which, fixed to the halved men's belts, would allow them to stand upright and move and even bend their bodies backwards and forwards, while the point kept firmly in the ground. Galateo the leper, who had been a gentleman when in health, acted as umpire; the Bad 'Un's seconds were Pamela's father and the chief constable, the Good 'Un's, two Huguenots. Dr. Trelawney stood by to lend his services, and arrived with a huge roll of bandages and a demijohn of balsam, as if to tend a battlefield. A lucky thing for me since he needed my help to carry all those things.

It was a greenish dawn; on the field the two thin black duelists stood still with swords at the ready. The leper blew his horn; it was the signal; the sky quivered like taut tissue; dormice in their lairs dug claws into soil, magpies with heads under wings tore feathers from their sides and hurt themselves, worms' mouths ate their own tails, snakes bit themselves with their own teeth, wasps broke their stings on stones, and everything turned against itself. Frost lay in wells, lichen turned to stone and stone to lichen, dry leaves to mold, and trees were filled by thick hard sap. So man moved against himself, both hands armed with swords.

Once again Pietrochiodo had done a masterly job. The compass legs made circles on the field and the duelers flung themselves into assaults of clanking metal and thudding wood, into feints and lunges. But they did not touch each other. At every lunge the sword's point seemed to go straight at the adversary's fluttering cloak, and each seemed determined to make for the part where there was nothing, that is the part where he should have been himself. Certainly if instead of half duelers there had been two whole ones, they would have wounded each other again and again. The Bad 'Un fought with fury and ferocity, yet never managed to launch his attacks just where his enemy was; the Good 'Un had correct mastery, but never did more than pierce the Viscount's cloak.

At a certain point they found themselves sword-guard to sword-guard; the points of their wooden legs were stuck in the ground like stakes. The Bad 'Un freed himself with a start and was just losing his balance and rolling to the ground when he managed to give a terrific swing not right on his adversary but very close; a swing parallel to the margin interrupting the Good 'Un's body, and so near that it was not clear at once if it was this side or the other.

But soon we saw the body under the cloak go purple with blood from head to groin and there was no more doubt. The Good 'Un swayed, but as he fell in a last wide, almost pitiful, movement he too swung his sword very near his rival, from head to abdomen, between the point where the Bad 'Un's body was not and the point where it might have been. Now the Bad 'Un's body also spouted blood along the whole length of the huge old wound; the lungs of both had burst all their vein ends and reopened the wound which had divided them in two. Now they lay face to face and the blood which had once been one man's alone again mingled in the field.

Aghast at this sight I had not noticed Trelawney; then I realized that the doctor was jumping up and down with joy on his grasshopper's legs, clapping his hands and shouting, "He's saved, he's saved! He's saved! Leave it to me."

Half an hour later we bore back one single wounded man on a stretcher to the castle. Bad and Good 'Uns had been tightly bound together; the doctor had taken great care to get all guts and arteries of both parts to correspond, and then a mile of bandages had tied them together so tightly that he looked more like an ancient embalmed corpse than a wounded man.

My uncle was watched night and day as he lay between life and death. One morning looking at that face crossed by a red line from forehead to chin and on down the neck, it was Sebastiana who first said, "There, he's moved."

A quiver was in fact going over my uncle's features, and the doctor wept for joy at seeing it transmitted from one cheek to the other.

Finally Medardo shut his eyes and his lips; at first his expression was lopsided; he had one eye frowning and the other supplicating, a forehead here corrugated and there serene, a mouth smiling in one corner and gritting its teeth in the other. Then gradually it became symmetrical again.

Dr. Trelawney said, "Now he's healed."

And Pamela exclaimed, "At last I'll have a husband with everything complete."

So my uncle Medardo became a whole man again, neither good nor bad, but a mixture of goodness and badness, that is, apparently not dissimilar to what he had been before the halving. But having had the experience of both halves each on its own, he was bound to be wise. He had a happy life, many children and a just rule. Our life too changed for the better. Some might expect that with the Viscount entire again, a period of marvelous happiness would open, but obviously a whole Viscount is not enough to make all the world whole.

Now Pietrochiodo built gibbets no longer, but mills, and Trelawney neglected his will-o'-the-wisps for measles and chickenpox. I, though, amid all this fervor of wholeness, felt myself growing sadder and more lacking. Sometimes one who thinks himself incomplete is merely young.

I had reached the threshold of adolescence and still hid among the roots of the great trees in the wood to tell myself stories. A pine needle could represent a knight, or a lady, or a jester. I made them move before my eyes and enraptured myself in interminable tales about them. Then I would be overcome with shame at these fantasies and would run off.

A day came when Dr. Trelawney left me too. One morning into our bay sailed a fleet of ships flying the British flag and anchored offshore. The whole of Terralba went to the seashore to look at them, except me, who did not know. The gunwales and rigging were full of sailors carrying pineapples and tortoises and waving scrolls with maxims on them in Latin and English. On the quarterdeck, amid officers in tricorn and wig, Captain Cook fixed the shore with his telescope, and as soon as he sighted Dr. Trelawney gave orders for him to be signaled by flag, "Come on board at once, Doctor, as we want to get on with that game of cards."

The doctor bade farewell to all at Terralba and left us. The sailors intoned an anthem, "Oh, Australia!" And the doctor was hitched on board astride a barrel of *cancarone*. Then the ships drew anchor.

I had seen nothing. I was deep in the wood telling myself stories. When I heard later, I began running towards the seashore crying, "Doctor! Doctor Trelawney! Take me with you! Doctor, you can't leave me here!"

But already the ships were vanishing over the horizon and I was left behind, in this world of ours full of responsibilities and will-o'-the-wisps.

About the Author

ITALO CALVINO's superb storytelling gifts earned him international renown and a reputation as "one of the world's best fabulists" (*New York Times Book Review*). He is the author of numerous works of fiction, as well as essays, criticism, and literary anthologies. Born in Cuba in 1923, Calvino was raised in Italy, where he lived most of his life. At the time of his death, in Siena in 1985, he was the most translated contemporary Italian writer.